"Fated Love"

A Lesbian Romance

Jenny Bloom

© 2020
Jenny Bloom

All rights reserved. No part of this publication may be reproduced, distributed, or transmitted in any form or by any means, including photocopying, recording, or other electronic or mechanical methods, without the prior written permission of the publisher, except in the case of brief quotations embodied in critical reviews and certain other non-commercial uses permitted by copyright law.

This book is intended for Adults (ages 18+) only. The contents may be offensive to some readers. It may contain graphic language, explicit sexual content, and adult situations. May contain scenes of unprotected sex. Please do not read this book if you are offended by content as mentioned above or if you are under the age of 18. Please educate yourself on safe sex practices before making potentially life-changing decisions about sex in real life.

This story is a work of fiction. Names, characters, businesses, places, events and incidents are the products of the author's imagination or used in a fictitious manner & are not to be construed as real. Any resemblance to actual persons, living or dead, or actual events is purely coincidental. Products or brand names mentioned are trademarks of their respective holders or companies. The cover uses licensed images & are shown for illustrative purposes only. Any person(s) that may be depicted on the cover are simply models.

Edition v1.00 (2020.07.20)
www.JennyBloomAuthor.com

Special thanks to the following volunteer readers who helped with proofreading: RB, Naomi W., Big Kid and those who assisted but wished to be anonymous. Thank you so much for your support.

Chapter One

"Another rejection," Amelia said, frustrated as she crumpled the piece of paper, tossing it to the side. This was the third one this week, and Amelia had no idea what to do about any of this.

It was getting ridiculous. Amelia hated that it was like this, and Amelia wanted to just find something right out of college. But, even after graduating with a degree in communications, trying to find some semblance of work in this world was proving to be much harder than she thought.

Amelia then looked at her emails. It was of course, another empty, barren land of nothing more than just a few coupons, and of course, emails saying they'll "Get back to her later" or some bullshit.

This wasn't going to work.

Amelia thought it would be easier. She did have a small gig working as a server, but it was different. It wasn't like she was actually getting much from that. Now, with bills, student loans, and god knows what else on the horizon, Amelia knew for a fact that this was definitely not the best thing for her to do right now.

Amelia needed something, anything.

That's when she noticed it. Amelia logged onto Facebook, reading the slew of people complaining, ignoring it, but then, she noticed an add.

"The Purple Panda," she said to herself.

It was a strip club that opened somewhat recently, and it had nothing but rave reviews. Their page was active, with people left and right looking at it. Amelia threaded her hands through her red hair, looking at herself.

Amelia was small, but she did have some flexibility. She wondered if this was something she could do. She knew how hard it was to get into this business, and it probably wasn't like she'd stand out or anything.

Or maybe she will. People like redheads.

Amelia looked at the page once more, and she clicked on the website. Amelia then noticed that there was a small space that talked about looking for new dancers.

It seemed too damn good to be true. Amelia definitely was curious about that. She quickly clicked on this, and she soon opened up a page with an application. She read it over, gazing at this, and as she looked at it, she realized what she must do.

"This is crazy, but it might work," she told herself.

She never did something like this before. Who knows if it would work? But her mom was getting onto her about not paying any share of the rent. She quickly typed in some of the information, pressing send. She said she wouldn't mind working during the day that way, she wouldn't get anything out of her mom.

When she pressed the send key, there was a strange feeling of relief as she did that. Maybe this was the work she'd been waiting for. If anything, too, she could be a server or something. Maybe she could get a night shift with that, so she didn't lose out on money.

Of course, she doubted this would get her anywhere. After all, it's not like she really had much of a chance.

But then, two days later, Amelia woke up, checking her email for something. After combing through the rejection emails from a couple of corporations, she quickly noticed one from The Purple Panda. She clicked on it, expecting rejection, but then, she read the contents.

Hello Amelia,

I must say, your resume is lacking, but that's fine. We'd like to extend an interview for a server job to you. If you're interested, please reply back with the appropriate time.

Thanks,

Mgmt.

Amelia read this, feeling excitement in her body. She didn't have experience, but there was something riveting about this. She quickly responded, saying sure, she'd love to come in. after pressing send, she wondered what might happen next.

What did fate have in store for her? what now? She grew curious of this.

The interview was set for Friday at 11 am. It was a little early, but Amelia didn't care. She wore a staid business suit, expecting to be overdressed when I got there.

I went to the address, but to my surprise, it was an establishment that looked far different from what I expected. I thought it might be a little bit run down or look like that, since that's the usual club feel. But instead, this place was dressed to the nines, contrasting with the area that it's in.

It was quite beautiful if I did say so myself. When I walked in, the club was quiet, but there were a couple of women dancing. Some of the men were there, dressed in staid business suits, but throwing money at the women.

Was it really all that easy?

To my surprise though, a familiar face appeared. When I saw a woman with long, jet-black hair and blue eyes come toward me, I realized my throat went dry from shock at the presence of this person.

"Kayla," I said when I saw her.

There was a small, devilish smile on her face, and when I noticed that, I immediately realized what type of world I was about to come into.

"Hey there Amelia, it's been a while," she said.

Suddenly, I realized that this was about to change me. Whether it's for the better or the worst is beside the point, but I certainly wondered what as well in the world might happen now, and exactly what type of job I was about to experience out here.

Chapter Two

Kayla smile, looking at Amelia. She was the same as always.

"You know, you were the last person I'd expect to get a job at a strip club Amelia," Kayla said with a smirk. She looked at Amelia, who was nervous as all hell.

It seemed very odd that Amelia wanted to work here. Kayla wondered if it was desperation. Of course, maybe she underestimated Amelia.

But Amelia was still just as pretty as she was back when they were in college together. It had been a few years, that's for sure, especially when Kayla ended up leaving abruptly.

She shook off those feelings. They were old times, a prior life, a prior abuser.

"Yeah well, being a college graduate isn't all it cracked up to be," Amelia said.

Kayla nodded.

"I imagine," she said.

There was an awkward silence, and Kayla tried to figure out how to change the subject.

"So uh, you know what is here, right? I don't want you to feel like you're getting into something you have no idea about, that's all," she said.

Amelia blushed, and Kayla had to admit, she had quite a cute face.

"Of course. I mean, I know it's weird and all, but I definitely understand what I'm doing here," she said.

Kayla smile, looking at her with an expectant grin.

"Tell you what, let's head over to the interview room. I'd rather not talk shop out here with, you know the dancers working and all," Kayla explained.

She trotted over to the area, with Amelia following suit. When they got inside, Kayla locked the door, sitting across from Amelia on the lounge chair.

"All right, so what do you know about this place?" Kayla said.

"It's a strip club, right? So that's...kind of what the women do here. I didn't know if I was going to be stripping or just serving right now," Amelia said.

Kayla paused. She wasn't against the idea of Amelia dancing, but it certainly might be hard for her at this point in time.

"I'm thinking more of a waitressing job. I mean, I'm still looking to hire you Amelia. Our last server had to quit. I found out that she was moving to Italy suddenly, so I needed to take over the serving duties. There's a couple of other women who were interested, and a couple who stepped up during the busy hours but having a server here for at least a few days during the week would be really nice for me. I'm trying to run a business, and would rather not do waitressing or dancing," Kayla said.

Amelia listened, and then nodded. She seemed to understand the situation at hand.

"So, what kind of work do I need to do here?" Amelia asked.

Kayla pulled out a whole handbook, giving it to here.

"It's simple really. We have a bar where those patrons who come in can order drinks, so you take them, and you give it to them. You may perform a little bit on stage, but that's really it. It's mostly a tipping system, but the men who come in here do know how to tip. I made this place one for the types of people who care about tipping services," Kayla said.

She made sure that, when the bar was opened, she chose the option of having people seek out the services which they desired. She was happy to offer these, and she could tell from the way that Amelia looked, this was exactly what she needed.

"I see. That sounds easy enough. People here aren't that weird, right?" Amelia asked.

Kayla chucked, imagining what weird must be to Amelia. She's seen it all, so it probably was a little bit different.

"Nah, most of the customers who come here know better than to harass the women who work here. Some of them get a little bit flirty, but that's really it. Simple stuff, really," she said.

"Thank God. I don't know if I could handle people like that," Amelia said.

"Yeah well, I try to make this place at least a little enjoyable for people. I did build this from the ground up, and I've seen so much," Kayla said.

That was putting it lightly. She never really wanted to subject others to the same thing she has. In a sense though, it did strengthen her, and make it possible for her to run a place like this. But, when Amelia looked at her with those big eyes, Kayla couldn't help but feel the urge to protect her.

"You've changed a lot since college Kayla,' Amelia said.

"How so?"

"I don't know, you just seem so strong, so sure of yourself. I'm a little jealous, really," Amelia admitted.

Kayla laughed at those words.

"Honey, you have nothing to be jealous of. I wish I could've finished school, but you know that wasn't possible. So, I made light of my situation. But I can see that you've changed a little bit too. Not the same old little timid self that you are," Kayla pointed out.

It was Amelia's turn to blush, and Kayla couldn't help but find it slightly adorable, and it definitely was a good thing to see.

"Yeah well, it's nice to see you again. Been a little bit, you know?" Amelia said.

"Indeed. So when can you start?"

Kayla hoped that Amelia would say right away. To her surprise though, Amelia spoke.

'Can I start tomorrow? I think tomorrow as a fresh start would be great," Amelia said.

"Sure. And if you want to, you can learn how to dance as well. I know the dancers make a crapload of cash," Kayla said. She did like that about her establishment. The women who worked here did take home some good money even after paying the club dues.

"Good, I'm glad. Cause ugh, I need it. Work sucks, even though I do have a degree. I thought it'd be better, but I guess not," Amelia admitted.

Kayla extended her arm, putting it on Amelia's shoulder.

"Hey, don't sweat it. It's not easy to get out in the world like this. I'm here for you. Remember, I'm still your friend despite being your boss," Kayla explained.

When she looked into Amelia's eyes, she felt a throbbing in her heart, a yearning for her. she wanted to be the person that she always knew she could be. Amelia nodded, grinning at her.

"Thank you Kayla. I appreciate it," she said.

"Not a problem. Know that I'm always here for you," Kayla said.

For a moment, she wanted to say something more. She forgot how damn cute Amelia was. In fact, it was hard not to hold back her feelings. But it was better this way.

Getting into the different aspects of her life with Amelia wasn't something she should do right now. She was her boss for Pete's sake. It wouldn't be a good look for her.

"Thanks for everything Kayla. I'll try to be the best waitress that I can for this place. And I want to make you proud," Amelia said.

"Very well. I'm excited to have you on the team," Kayla said.

She got the rest of the paperwork out, mostly waiver forms saying she's not responsible for any stupid stunts pulled at the establishment. As she offered Amelia a pen, they brushed fingers, causing Kayla to flush. She didn't really talk much to Amelia during college, but they did know one another from the classes. Still, the fact that she was here now, after all of this, felt quite different.

"I'm glad that you're here," Kayla said.

"Same here. You've saved my ass. I hope this works out," Amelia said.

"Oh, and you'll probably want to work during the daytime, right? I know that you still live with your mom and it might be weird and such," Kayla said.

Amelia paused, and then, she sighed.

"I can do like second shift. My mom doesn't really ask about this sort of thing, she just wants me working right now," Amelia said.

Kayla paused, thinking about what to do. She then nodded.

"Fair enough. I'll put you down for second shift then. I'm excited to get you started Amelia," she said.

Amelia finished up her paperwork and headed out, closing the door behind her. Kayla went over to the bar, getting a couple of drinks for the patrons, but thankful that she'll have someone new taking over this in a day or so.

"I can't wait to run my club like how I want to," she said.

However, Kayla kept thinking about Amelia, how pretty she was, and how gorgeous she'd look on stage. Kayla was learning to dance too and knew a thing or two, but she wondered if one day Amelia would perform.

She hoped so. It would probably be a nice little thing for her, and for Kayla, it certainly would be nice to behold, that's for sure.

Course, that was down the line, and right now, Kayla needed to keep her eyes on the prize, and ignore the voicemails she got from certain people at the club.

Chapter Three

Amelia felt so different just from spending a few mere moments with Kayla.

It was different. Kayla was gorgeous, and Amelia did like the time that she spent with her. but, something about this felt different. Instead of being happy that she got a job, she felt like she made a life change.

Oh well, it's not like she was complaining or anything. Amelia made her way back home, and when she got there, she saw her mother at her desk, working hard.

"Hey Mom," she said.

"Hey. So, how's the new job," she said.

Amelia paused, trying to figure out how to explain this to her mom without it raising suspicion.

"Oh, it's good that's all. I got it actually," she said.

"I see. So, it did work out like that. I'm surprised," she said.

"What do you mean?" Amelia asked.

"Oh nothing, I'm just surprised you landed something so fast. What is it exactly?" her mother inquired.

Amelia tried her best to figure out the best excuse she possibly could. She knew her mom would hound her if she didn't speak the truth, but the last thing Amelia wanted was to make things weird for her.

"Well, I'm serving at a local club. I'll be giving alcohol to the patrons there," Amelia said.

She hoped more than anything her mom wouldn't say no to any of this or make things worse. But, to her surprise, her mother shrugged.

"Seems fair. It won't be any seedy location or anything, correct?" she asked.

Amelia shook her head.

"No, I know the owner. She was someone I met a few years back," Amelia explained.

"I see. Well, just be careful. And don't work for any of those disgusting strip clubs or anything. They're gross and you're going to carry a disease home if you do," her mother chimed.

Amelia felt a bit of a sting from those words. She didn't think strip clubs were bad or anything, but every time Amelia got a job, her mom would always say the same thing. She was curious about this, simply because she didn't find those establishments gross for the most part. They were a business offering a service, that's all.

"Why do you dislike strip clubs so much mom? You always bring it up whenever I say I'm potentially getting a new job. So, what the hell gives?" Amelia asked.

Her mother tensed at those words, eyes daring about. She put her hand through her red hair, which was brighter than Amelia's own. She looked at Amelia with concern on her face.

"I'm just doing what's best for you," she said.

"Yeah but that doesn't answer why—"

"It's none of your business Amelia," her mother snapped.

The look on her face screamed that it was time for Amelia to take her leave, which she did. She didn't understand why her mother was so against strip clubs. Unless of course, she had a bad experience in one.

And even so, it wasn't like Amelia was going out every night to one. She worked there, and the establishment seemed very friendly. Its empowered women. None of the women there looked to be in poor shape or anything. If anything, they looked better than your average factory workers.

"Anyway, I'm going to head up to my room. I've got to prepare for tomorrow. I start during second shift," Amelia said.

Her mother clicked here tongue.

"Very well. If you can, head the store and get some more food for us. We're almost out of milk," she said.

Amelia nodded.

"Will do Mom," she said.

Amelia headed over to her room to get her wallet. She couldn't wait for these bills to magically go away. She wondered how good she'd be at this sort of job. After all, it was a bit different from the usual jobs that she had, but it wasn't like Amelia was really complaining either. She wouldn't mind a nice little change of pace.

Things felt like they were looking up, and although Amelia was worried about tomorrow, she wasn't as nervous as she should be. She had a good feeling about this.

Still, something about this felt so different, and almost unreal in a sense. For Amelia, she was just happy to have a job. But, when she did see Kayla there, something changed within her.

Instead of feeling regret about it all, she felt happy in a sense. She felt like...they could see one another again.

It was no lie that Amelia did like women, and she did admit, she had a crush on Kayla. Even though she'd never tell her directly, saying that to her would make Amelia happier than ever. But she didn't want to jinx what they already had, and she didn't want to make things awkward.

Still, it certainly made things hard, at least for them.

"I wish this was easier," Amelia said.

She didn't know whether or not Kayla felt the same, or if it would work out. She did wonder how work would be. She did remember Kayla looking her over as soon as she came in, obviously checking her out.

It wasn't like she was against it at all, that's for sure. Amelia felt a bit nervous about starting but there was something about all of this which made her happy and satisfied.

It was a matter of how tomorrow went, but Amelia had a feeling that it would only get better from there.

Chapter Four

Kayla saw Amelia come in first thing that afternoon in the uniform, and for a second, Kayla felt her entire professionalism go out the window as she stared at Amelia.

She looked hot. The uniform, which was a cropped top and a miniskirt, hugged her curves. Of course, Kayla had on a big jacket and some shorts on underneath, no doubt to hide from her mom who probably would blow a gasket if she saw her like this.

"There you are,"

"Hey, sorry for being late. My mom kept bothering me with things," Amelia said.

"Oh, it's fine, I just started taking care of things here. Anyway, you ready to work?" Kayla said.

She had a feeling that today would be interesting. She wondered how the people here would respond to the new server.

"Sure, but what do I do?" she asked.

"First, you'll stay at the bar for the most part. If someone comes up and orders a drink, you'll make it. I made a nice little cheat sheet of all the drinks that you'll need to make there," she said, pointing at the little piece of paper there.

Kayla watched as Amelia pored over it, looking at it with interest and shaky hands.

"Relax, it's a slow period, so we probably won't have a bunch of drinks. You also can go around and ask if people want drinks. But I do suggest doing it in a way that won't annoy the crap out of others, because lots of people are weird about being bothered. Neither of these guys have been asked though, so I suggest trying now," Kayla said.

"Okay," Amelia said, feeling a bit shaky.

"Oh, and also take off those shorts. I know it's awkward, but it'll get you more tips," Kayla said with a wink.

"Oh, okay," Amelia said.

She took them off, leaving them with her jacket, and then, she grabbed the pen and paper. She walked on over to the patron sitting in the corner, staring at the woman who was dancing.

"Excuse me sir, would you like a drink?" Amelia asked.

The guy whipped his head around, looking at her. Kayla stood nearby in case there was anything wrong. She expected the guy to say something crude, but then, he smiled.

"Oh yes please, a rum and coke would be wonderful. So, are you the new girl working here? I heard Kayla was looking for new talent," he said.

His voice was soothing and sweet, but Kayla could see Amelia standing there like a deer in headlights.

"Yeah, this is one of my new girls. I hope you take a liking to her, because I'd like to give the reins of drinks to someone else. It gets tiring doing all of that all the time," Kayla said.

"Indeed. Well, she's quite a looker there Kayla. Nice job," he said with a wink.

Kayla looked over at Amelia, who was flush crimson.

"Thank you, sir. Anyway, I better get this girl back to where she belongs. She's a complete deer in headlights right now," Kayla said.

She brought Amelia back, sitting her down over by the bar.

"All right, now you must make a rum and coke. Want to make that yourself?" Kayla said.

"Yeah," Amelia said.

Kayla put her hand on Amelia's shoulder, flashing her a grin.

"Stop being so nervous. Guys love a confident woman here in these parts. So definitely try to exude that," she said with a smile on her face.

The intent of that was of course to help Amelia get over her stage fright. But, the obvious blush on her face said so much more.

"Thank you so much Kayla. You're too good to me," she said with a smile.

"Relax, will you? I know it's scary, but trust me on this Amelia, you'll rock at this. I'm so excited to have you on board," she said.

Kayla wasn't just trying to amp the confidence up,. She really did want Amelia to do well with this. It was novel to both of them, working together like this, but she noticed that Amelia was a bit different after that pep talk.

"I will. Thank you Kayla. You know, even after college you seem to know exactly what to say at the right time, she said.

It was Kayla's turn to blush at this point, flushing at the words that were said.

"No problem. Get on with it. Go give him that drink and show him how it's done!" Kayla said.

She watched as Amelia walked over, trying to exude a feeling of confidence as she gave the drink to the man. Kayla stood off to the side, watching the fallout, hoping more than anything she didn't have to step in.

To her surprise though, the man grinned at her, a beaming smile that took both of them by surprise.

"Thank you so much dear. You certainly have a lot of potential. I'm impressed, and that's definitely saying it lightly," he said.

"Really," Amelia asked.

"Course. You definitely have the potential to work here, and I'm sure that Kayla over here sees it too," he said.

Kayla smiled, walking over and patting her on the back.

"Of course, I'll train her nice and well for all of you," she said with a purr.

"Ahh yes. What I wouldn't give to see her dance however," he said.

Kayla blushed, but then, she smiled.

"We're getting to that point. For now, I need a server, not a dancer. Got plenty of those," she said.

"Indeed. Well, I'm excited to report to my friends about the new hire you have Kayla. Well done," he said.

He went back to enjoying the women , and soon, Kayla stepped near the bar. She saw another man raise his hand, and she watched as Amelia went over to take the drinks. Fr Kayla, this was both fun to watch, but also interesting. She blushed as she saw Amelia handle the drinks like a pro.

"God she's good," she said.

Kayla felt proud of this. She knew that Amelia would fit right in, but of course, seeing her body move around, the way the skirt moved upwards, exposing her backside just slightly, it was enough to make Kayla stop and stare for a while, completely immersed in the way she looked.

No, she couldn't do that. It was taboo.

But it was still wonderful to look at, and she'd be lying if she wasn't interested in Amelia.

Chapter Five

Working at the club was different from a normal serving job.

For starters, starting in the afternoon wasn't all that bad. Amelia had the early customers, who of course came in in-between meetings and the like.

Then she got a taste of the night shift, which was a whole different breed. From the customers, to even the strippers, it felt like a whole different world out there it wasn't necessarily a bad thing, but at the same time, Amelia wasn't used to any of this.

Some of the women weren't all that happy with a new person working, even though Amelia didn't have anything to do with dancing. Maybe it was because the men took the tips away and the women would have to pay out to the server, but a couple of women gave death glares to Amelia for the first couple weeks of working.

But, Kayla wasn't having it. Her tall, demanding structure was enough to ward off a couple of complaints.

"Don't let them bother you, Amelia. If anyone gives you trouble, have them come to me," Kayla said.

Amelia flushed whenever Kayla stood up for her, or even helped her. It made her feel a little bit nervous, but at the same time, she kind of liked it. She felt like she could rely on Kayla in her own way, even though she had no idea how this would work out in the future.

For Kayla, it didn't seem like Amelia was a burden. Amelia would ask if she was okay, and Kayla would always be there, with the same words, and the same smile.

"No, I'm great Amelia. Trust me, I'm happy to have you around," she said.

Amelia actually felt that. She felt wanted and appreciated here, which was different from the prior serving jobs. Those prior jobs were so different. They only cared about making money and not much else.

But Amelia actually enjoyed working here, and she came in more and more than she usually did. Of course, whenever Amelia would leave, her mom would always look up, stopping her.

"You're leaving again?"

"Yeah Mom. I'm going to head to the club," she said.

"Fine. Just be safe," she muttered, heading back to work.

Amelia felt a bit of regret lying to her mom. Well, it wasn't necessarily lying as hiding the truth. But she knew that her mom was the type to freak out, so having things like this was...easier in a sense.

Amelia didn't feel like she was hiding who she really was when she was at the club. She could be herself, even if it meant being someone a little bit different.

And of course, not to mention the uniform was so different from the server outfits she wore in the past. Most of the time, she wore staid little suits or a shirt and pants. But here, it was miniskirts and crop tops, which of course got her tips since she had sizable breasts.

Amelia did feel a little embarrassed every time some man would ogle her, but then, she'd look over at Kayla who had her eye on her in a protective manner. Amelia felt like, even if things go hairy, Kayla would bail her out.

One night, after a long day at the club, Kayla cleaned up the space. Amelia sat next to her, helping to count not just the club revenue, but the tips too.

"Wow, we made a lot tonight," Amelia said.

"Yeah, welcome to Fridays Amelia. It's always like this," Kayla said.

"I see. So...would it be good for me to work then?" she asked.

"Listen, work however much you want. This is your job. I have my hours and I've worked hard to bring this club to the level it's at. It's your choice on how much you want to do," Kayla said.

Amelia paused. A part of her wanted to work more hours. After all, this was something she very much enjoyed. But she definitely didn't want to burden herself.

"It's all right. I actually might. just got to make it look like I'm working normal hours to my mom. That's all," she said.

Kayla looked up at her, and Amelia could tell there was something amiss.

"How is your mom by the way? I remembered meeting her one time during that project. She seems nice. Little overbearing, but cool," Kayla said.

"I mean, I wouldn't necessarily say cool. If she found out I was working in a strip club, even as a server, she'd kill me. I don't even get naked, but she probably would think it's something terrible," Amelia said.

"Why, do you want to dance?" Kayla asked.

Amelia flushed, looking at her.

"N-not really. Nothing personal Kayla, I'm just not comfy with that. I kind of prefer serving. It's my comfy space," she said.

Kayla laughed, lightly pulling her in.

"Relax, I'd never make you do something you're not *comfy* with. I'm surprised she agreed to you working here. Does she think you work at a bar or something?" she asked.

"Somewhat. I also kind of lie and say I'm out with friends when I get back late," Amelia said.

Kayla nodded.

"I see. Well, I do suggest eventually getting away from that. Having a parent hound you like that isn't all that healthy," Kayla said.

Amelia knew that's what she needed to do, but she wasn't ready for it yet.

"It's easier said than done, you know," she pointed out.

Kayla looked at her, nodding in agreement.

"Oh, I know honey. I very much know. I don't speak to my dad for that reason," she stated.

The tone of her voice alone was enough to make Amelia regret saying anything.

"I'm sorry Kayla. I didn't want you to feel bad," she said.

Kayla stopped, and Amelia wondered fi she said something to piss her off.

"Nah, it's just difficult to discuss, that's all," she admitted.

Amelia nodded.

"I don't hate you for not talking about this," Amelia said. She wanted to at least bridge the gap.

"Thanks Amelia. I know you don't. I'd rather not speak on it, but make sure you're happy with what you do in life. All I'm saying," she said.

Before Amelia could ask anything more, Kayla finished cleaning up the area. When she went over to look at the money made, she smiled.

"Well I'll have rent and then some," she said.

"Really?"

"Yep. Say, why don't we hang out at some point down the line Amelia? I'll take you out to dinner. My treat," Kayla said.

Amelia flushed. She couldn't believe Kayla actually wanted to do that.

"Yeah, but how? Who will cover?" Amelia asked.

"I have someone who comes in a few times a month to relieve me. This baby is my pride and joy, but sometimes a mom needs a break too," Kayla said with a smirk.

The smile on her face made Amelia's heart thump. She then grinned at Kayla, feeling comfortable with her words.

"Then it's a date," she said.

Kayla gave her a teasing smile.

"Good, because I was afraid what may happen if you say no," she retorted.

The two of them teased and laughed, feeling comfy around one another. Amelia wondered if there was a way to tell Kayla how she felt.

Nah, that would make things awkward. It wouldn't work out anyway.

Chapter Six

Spending time with Amelia was probably Kayla's favorite thing about this job. It wasn't just the time that they spent training and working together. Amelia would spend her after-hours with Kayla, and Kayla loved that she didn't feel alone in many of these cases. They sat around and talked, even when it was way after hours.

For Kayla, having Amelia around was so different. It was a breath of fresh air, something that she needed, and something she felt Amelia needed to.

They agreed to hang out the next Friday they could get off, which was a week from now. Kayla called up the partner she had in the business, her friend Mandy. While Mandy preferred to work on her other business, she'd step in and help Kayla as needed.

"Hey girl," she said.

"Hey Mandy, it's me. Listen, I know that we usually don't do this, but is there a way you can take over my Friday night? I wanted to hang out with someone. I promised that we'd spend a little bit of time together," Kayla said.

She hoped Mandy would listen. There was a chuckle, and then, Mandy spoke.

"Course. So, who's the lucky girl," she teased.

Kayla blushed slightly in response, having trouble saying the words she wanted to for but a moment. After a second, she took a deep breath.

"Well, it's just a friend, but who knows. Maybe it'll become something more," Kayla said.

"Of course. I'll gladly run the show. I've been meaning to come over lately as well, just the business has been a little crazy on my end. Lots of people demanding things out of me, so I've been working on that," she explained.

"Totally understandable. Thank you so much," Kayla said.

"Not a problem! I definitely don't want to leave you hanging," she said.

Kayla smiled to herself. She was grateful for Mandy's help, even in times like this. After they hung up, Kayla gave Amelia a call, explaining everything.

"Are you sure?" Amelia asked.

"Damn sure. I'd love to take you out," she said.

"Sure. I wouldn't mind that," Amelia replied.

The affirmation was enough to make Kayla smile. Things were definitely better these days, and she wasn't regretting all of this.

For Kayla, this was the beginning of something more, something bigger, and for her, she definitely wasn't regretting a damn thing agreeing to any of this. She felt happy knowing she could take Amelia out like this. They didn't just have to spend time together after hours at the club.

It felt refreshing once she met up with Amelia at the restaurant. They agree it was probably better to meet here than anywhere else, given the way Amelia's mom was. Kayla wished that Amelia could get away from her, but it may not happen for a long time.

She was also just happy that Amelia was actually meeting her period. After they said their greetings, Kayla reached in, giving Amelia a hug.

"I was thinking we could check this place out. My treat" she offered.

"Sure," Amelia said.

They walked into the restaurant, stepping in and checking out the place. As they sat, the server came on by to get drinks. Kayla ordered a bottle of red wine for the table, and after the server came over with it and poured it, they disappeared, leaving both Amelia and her alone.

"All right, well now that we're both away from work, we can actually have a normal relationship together," Kayla said.

Amelia smiled, blushing slightly.

"Yeah, we can. You know, I've always liked you Kayla. I didn't want to make things weird though back in college," Amelia said.

Kayla chuckled, sipping her wine for but a moment before speaking.

"You'll need to do a lot to make things weird Amelia. Trust me, I deal with a lot on the daily already," she said.

Amelia nodded.

"That's true. So, what made you want to go into this business? What made you want to open a strip club? Not that it's a problem or anything," Amelia said.

Kayla thought about it. Should she tell Amelia the truth, that it wasn't really her choice, but instead, the circumstances she was thrown into? That this was a spur-of-the-moment idea to make some quick cash to get away from the abuse?

"It's a bit of a long story. Let's just say that things weren't all that great, and it was either figure out a solution and work with what you have, or just give into the abuse. There's a reason why I don't speak with my family much anymore," Kayla said.

"Yeah. I mean my mom doesn't know anything, but god, sometimes I wish she would just take the damn hint," Amelia said.

"It's not easy for people to do that my dear. Most people are blind to it, and if you're not careful, you definitely will get hurt. I mean, I kind of hope that one day your mom comes around, but I'm not holding my breath," Kayla said.

She knew Amelia's mom. The one time she met her, the lady was nothing more than rude and crass. She didn't have the energy to deal with someone like that. But, when Kayla looked at Amelia, seeing how cute she was, Kayla wondered if there was anything more, she could do.

"Yeah, my mom is kind of an asshole. Luckily, she's kind of distanced herself from everything. I worry that one day, she'll learn everything and then kick me out. I don't want that, but I'm actually ready for that if it does happen," Amelia admitted.

Kayla wished there was something which she could do, something to make all of this a little easier on all of them. But she didn't know what else was out there.

"I mean, if you ever need anything I'm here to help. I know I'm far from perfect, but just know I'm here for you," Kayla insisted.

Amelia nodded, and Kayla could see the smile on her face.

"Thanks for everything Kayla. Seriously. You gave me a job when nobody else would, and you're so sweet too. It's...refreshing really. In the past, I was always stuck with trying to make things right when in reality it just didn't work out like that. But you care about me, and you want to do what's best for me. Which is a nice thing to have. So, thanks," Amelia said.

"You're welcome Amelia. You know, I would've helped out sooner if it weren't for everything that happened. But now that I'm free from that life, I feel like a new woman," she admitted.

Kayla didn't like thinking about her past. It was far too hard for her to come to terms with. But, if she could at least make one person happy, whether it be Amelia, or someone else, it would make everything worth it.

"You're definitely a breath of fresh air in all of this Kayla," Amelia said.

"What do you mean?" Kayla said.

"I've been pressed for a job. I've been in deb for far too long. But now that I have a job where it pays well, I feel like I can actually do something with my life. It's really nice," Amelia admitted.

Kayla smile.

"Yeah, I'm glad that you can find something. Makes me not regret going back to college though. I thought I needed it, but judging from the way things are for you, I don't think I really do," she said.

"You really don't Kayla. You've got a great business anyway. The dancers are actually nice at your establishment, something I was expecting to run into when I worked there. But, after they realized I was here to stay, they all started to tolerate me a bit more," Amelia said.

"Yeah. I don't want to come forward with our relationship yet. I think it's best if we keep everything under wraps for now," Kayla said.

With the people on her back, the last thing she needed was them to come around and try to harass her for everything. Plus, with the way Amelia's mom was, it would only be worse if they were out right now.

For now, things needed to stay chill.

"I'm glad we can spend time together though. I was a little worried about that. It seems like there's a lot going on in your life," Amelia admitted.

Kayla nodded.

"Yeah. Just people from my past. Stuff I need to settle with them. I'm trying to get the club to the point where they have no reason to bother me. But of course, that's far easier said than done, you know," she admitted.

"Yeah, I feel that. Well, you're doing a great job. I'm glad to be a part of your team. And...I've considered dancing. I wouldn't mind learning how at some point," Amelia said.

Kayla wouldn't mind seeing that. After all, Amelia had a nice body, and a super cute face. She felt like a lucky as hell woman to have her here.

"I'll see if there is any way I can get you a couple dancing gigs. If that's cool with you," she said.

Amelia beamed. "That's perfect. Thank you so much Kayla. You're amazing!"

Kayla didn't think she was that great, but the reassurance was worth it.

"Nah, I'm just trying to make things easier for both of us. But thank you Amelia. For being there for me," she said.

"You're welcome. I definitely love working for you and being a part of the team in my own way," Amelia said.

For the rest of dinner, they spent time talking about their past. Although Kayla didn't discuss her own hardships, she was happy to talk with Amelia a little bit about everything going on. There was something refreshing about all of this. After dinner, they walked out into the parking lot, but when they got out there, Amelia stopped.

"By the way, there is something I wanted to do Kayla," she said.

"What is it?"

Before Kayla could say anything more, Amelia leaned in, pressing her lips to Kayla's own. She kissed Kayla gingerly for a little bit, and then, Kayla eagerly responded. For a second, neither of them moved away from one another in the parking lot, spending their time together for a brief moment. When Amelia pulled back, she looked at Kayla with a reddened face.

"Thanks. I wanted to give that to you," she said.

"Same here. I've wanted to do that for a little bit. Since that one time we worked on that group project in college," she admitted.

Kayla didn't know what this would turn into, but when Amelia kissed her, it made her feel like maybe, just maybe, this was what she'd been looking for. Although things were still in the formative stages,

Kayla enjoyed this, and so did Amelia. They'd make this work, even in their own way.

Chapter Seven

For Amelia, kissing Kayla was something she'd wanted to do for a little while, but she didn't want to make things weird for either of them. But, upon kissing Kayla, she realized that Kayla felt the same way, and the touch of Kayla's lips against her own made Amelia realize that the feelings were definitely mutual.

They spent a good five minutes in the parking lot kissing, both of them feeling the excitement and thrill from one another's mouth. The feeling of Kayla's lips on her own was riveting, and Amelia definitely enjoyed everything about this.

The touch of their lips, the fire against one another, the sensation of this, it was all too amazing, and Amelia wanted nothing more than to experience all of this, and let things continue like this.

They stayed in the parking lot for what felt like forever, both of them excited and experiencing all of this. It was definitely an amazing moment, and Amelia would stop at nothing to have more of this.

Both of them moaned against one another's lips, tasting, teasing and experiencing one another. Until finally, Kayla pulled away, looking at her dead in the eye.

"Are you all right?" she asked.

"Yeah. Why?" Amelia asked, flushing crimson.

"I was thinking we could take this back to my place," she offered.

Amelia flushed, feeling her body hot with need. She didn't expect to get this for with Kayla, but here she was, being taken back for more fun with her.

"Sure. I'd love that," she said.

Kayla smiled, opening up the car door and slipping inside. Amelia did the same, and son, Kayla started the car. After a few minutes, they ended up at her place, which was close to the club.

"You're not far from work," Amelia said.

"Yeah, I did that for a reason. Wanted to keep myself close," she pointed out.

Amelia nodded. It made sense.

"Let's go inside then," she said. Amelia had no idea how this all went. Kayla then smiled at her, extending her hand.

"Is this your first time?"

Amelia blushed in response to those words.

"H-how did you know?" she inquired.

"It's simple, really. I can see it in your eyes. You're nervous about all of this, and you're frightened. But you really don't have to be afraid," she admitted.

Amelia nodded, feeling the anxiety skyrocket, and her whole body feel on edge.

"O-Okay," she said.

They walked inside, and when Kayla unlocked the door, Amelia slipped in. as soon as she did, Kayla moved forward, capturing their lips once again.

Amelia let Kayla take the lead, kissing her back, enjoying the sensation of this. Kayla smiled, kissing her back and enjoying all of this. The two of them spent what felt like forever kissing and experiencing the fire against one another, moaning one another's name in response to the touches.

Amelia felt like she was experiencing a whole new world when they kissed. Kayla seemed to know exactly what she was doing, kissing Amelia with a passion. Amelia responded, making out with her, and the two of them stayed like that for a long time, neither of them stopping either. It was amazing, almost mesmerizing, and Amelia couldn't help but feel her whole body ignite with need.

Suddenly, Amelia was pushed against the wall, and soon, she started to feel Kayla's tongue against Amelia's lips, begging for entrance. Amelia was starstruck, shocked by how it felt. Suddenly, Kayla pulled away, flushing.

"Are you…good?" she asked.

"Yeah. Sorry, I'm just surprised, that's all. I'm not mad or anything though," Amelia sad.

Kayla smiled, and soon, they began kissing again. Kayla pushed her tongue forward, asking for entrance to Amelia's lips once more. Amelia then started to open her mouth, and soon, she let Kayla's tongue into there, mingling and touching it as well.

The two of them moaned against one another, feeing the passions form both their bodies grow in a way that was different from what they experienced before. For Amelia, this was the beginning of something new, something amazing, and she loved the ay Kayla felt against her.

Kayla then moved Amelia over to the couch, pushing her down slightly. Amelia let out a breathy gasp, feeling a flush of embarrassment ghost over her face. Kayla then started to kiss her again, but then moved her lips over toward Amelia's neck, lightly pressing her lips there, touching them slightly.

Amelia let out a cry, feeling everything change over time. She couldn't help but let out a small cry of excitement and pleasure, enjoying the way that this felt. Amelia then started to feel Kayla press her lips there, sucking on the flesh and causing Amelia to let out a small moan of excitement.

It was like heaven on earth for Amelia. Although it was sensitive, at the same time, the kisses were sensual. Amelia felt Kayla continue to trail her lips downwards until she got toward her collarbone. She then moved forward, looking at Amelia.

It was an implicit sign, one asking if Amelia was cool with this.

Amelia nodded, giving her the okay to continue with this.

For Kayla, it was obvious that Amelia's agreement changed something in her. Amelia felt Kayla start to let out a small gasp, pushing her hands toward Amelia's shirt, moving it off, over her head. Amelia blushed, feeling eyes on her as Kayla moved her hands toward Amelia's breasts, touching them slightly through the fabric.

Amelia had small breasts, and she felt like Kayla's eyes were on them. Kayla was much more endowed, but she was a bit thicker, and it made sense in a way.

Amelia felt Kayla's lips move downwards, touching her collarbone and touched the tip of the area with her tongue. She then moved her hands to Amelia's bra, undoing the clasp and letting it fall downwards.

Amelia flushed, feeling exposed by the way she looked. Amelia could feel her heart racing, and Kayla smiled at her, touching her chin.

"Relax. I have you," she said.

Amelia felt reassured by that. Suddenly, Kayla moved her hands toward the tip of Amelia's nipple, touching it slightly with her lips. Amelia let out a cry, bucking her hips and moaning in response.

"H-holy crap," she said.

"You good?" Kayla asked.

"Y-yeah, I am," she admitted, blushing crimson.

"You need to relax Amelia. Trust me," Kayla said.

Amelia blushed, but she felt like all eyes were on her. She never felt this much stimulation before, but in a strange way, she really liked it. She could feel Kayla's lips move toward her nipple, taking the bud in her mouth and sucking on it, causing Amelia to let out a small cry, bucking her hips and moaning in response.

Amelia felt like she was at the mercy of Kayla's touches, and in a sense, she liked it. Kayla moved her lips over the other bud, sucking on it a bit harder, flicking her tongue around the ring of her nipple before letting it rest over the edge of the bud. She then pressed her fingers toward the tip of Amelia's other bud, not neglecting it in the least, and Amelia cried out, pushing her body upwards, enjoying the sensation of this.

It was the perfect moment, and Amelia couldn't help but love everything about this. She definitely was happy about it, and she knew that Kayla was enjoying this as well. Kayla continued to touch and tease both nipples, letting her tongue move over and mingle toward the tip of it, pressing there slightly, pulling on the bud. For Amelia, this was like heaven on earth, and she thoroughly enjoyed every moment of this.

Amelia was lost in the touches, but then, she felt Kayla's hands move toward the apex of her pants, cupping her heat. Amelia felt her eyes boggle out of her head, causing her to tense up, moaning in response, enjoying the sensation of everything which was happening.

She was sensitive, and Kayla seemed to have a liking to that. She lightly teased Amelia through her pants, causing Amelia to let out a series of moans and cries.

"You want more?" she asked Amelia in a sensual manner, touching the very tip of her earlobe with her breath. Amelia shuddered, crying out loud in both pleasure, and desire.

"Y-yes," she said.

Amelia watched as Kayla's hands moved toward her pants, undoing the fly that was there and slipping her pants all the way down. Amelia blushed, feeling slightly surprised by it all, and soon, Kayla's hands moved toward the very tip of her pussy, teasing her clit with small, sensual touches through her panties.

Amelia's body was on fire. She cried out in pleasure, feeling completely enthralled by all of this. Amelia watched as Kayla slipped her hands to each side of her panties, pulling them all the way downwards, watching as Amelia's eyes started to widen in shock and surprise. She then watched as Kayla started to lightly tease her pussy, starting with her clit, using her tongue to touch and flick there. Amelia gripped the edge of the couch, shivering in delight, feeling at the mercy of her touches and teases.

She was a natural. Amelia felt like she was being serviced by a total queen. The way her fingers pumped into her warm cavern, the way her lips seemed to move in perfect synchronization with her hands, all of this was right there, and Amelia felt like she was in a whole new world like this.

It was heavenly, it was divine, and dammit, she was going to experience this whole moment right then and there, enjoying the sensations that were happening at this present moment.

Amelia was losing control. Her fingers moved faster and faster, touching and teasing every single movement, letting her hands grip and control there. As she did that, Amelia started to feel her body tense up, her whole pussy tighten with desire and need, and suddenly, as quickly as it happened, she then cried out, feeling her entire body tense up, stop, and then, she released.

She let out a small series of sounds as Kayla finished there. She then pulled out, looking at Amelia with a smile.

"Everything okay?" she asked.

Amelia nodded.

"Yeah. It's your turn though,' she said.

It was Kayla's turn to blush, and Amelia couldn't help but find it cute.

"O-okay. Are you sure? I don't want you to—"

Before Kayla could finish those words, Amelia was between her legs, pulling her panties down with a quick, almost furious motion. She then moved her hands over toward Kayla's panties, pulling them downwards, exposing her to Amelia.

Amelia tried to do as Kayla did, pressing her lips there, touching and teasing in the same way. It seemed to work. Kayla grabbed her head, holding it there. Amelia pressed her fingers inside, pumping three of them in almost a furry of motions. She couldn't help but love the way that Kayla sounded, the little moans and screams that uttered from her lips making Amelia flush, feeling hot as she did this to Kayla.

She continued to touch her hands there, moving in and out, in and out, and it was then, after a few more motions, she turned her hands upwards, pushing them there, letting them rest against the very edge of the sweet spot. When she hit that part of her warm cavern, she watched as Kayla started to tense up, crying out, and soon, she then pushed herself forward, and then back.

Amelia tasted her release on her lips, pulling back and licking them. She smiled at Kayla with a smirk.

"Have fun?"

"Oh yes. You're a natural Amelia. I thought you did this before," she admitted.

Amelia blushed, but then, she quickly shook her head.

"No, I learned from you of course," she said.

Kayla then smiled, touching her hair and rustling it.

"Well, you're a goddamn natural," she teased.

She then gave Amelia a long, passionate kiss and Amelia couldn't help but feel good and happy about it all. Despite how things were, and how they could be, she was happy to have Kayla by her side.

Of course, if her mother finds out about this, she'll be in deep trouble.

But of course, that's if her mother finds out about it, which Amelia planned to keep away for long enough. But, how long would that be?

It would only be a matter of time before she found out.

Chapter Eight

After they had sex, Kayla pulled Amelia into her arms, cuddling on the couch with her.

"Are you doing okay?" Kayla asked.

"Yeah, I'm wonderful. What about you though, you seem like you're on edge about something," Amelia said.

Dammit. Amelia was better at reading her than she thought.

"It's nothing. I'm just a little worried about the club. That's all," she said.

"Why are you worried about the club?" Amelia asked.

Was it the time to tell her? Kayla paused, hesitating for a second.

"I don't want to worry you or anything Amelia," she said.

Amelia looked at her with a frown, a look of disappointment easily on her eyes.

"You're lying. Something is wrong, and you're just afraid to admit it," Amelia pointed out.

Kayla didn't know how much longer she could go keep on lying to Amelia.

"It's nothing, really. I swear," she said to Amelia.

Of course, that was an outright lie. She knew that if the mess with her father wasn't taken care of, things could get ugly.

But Amelia didn't stop there. She pulled away, looking at Kayla with a serious look.

"If you need to take care of something, then please do so," she said. Amelia meant it too, and Kayla could tell by the serious look on her face.

"I'm trying Amelia, but I'd rather you not get sucked into this. It's affairs of the club, just worried about how things will go from here on out. It's a personal problem that's lasted a while, so I definitely think that it was only a matter of time," Kayla explained.

Amelia nodded, and she soon stepped back.

"Well, if you need to take care of anything, please do so. I mean, I know it's a little ironic of me to be saying that given my situation, but I definitely don't 'want you suffering as well," she pointed out.

Kayla nodded, feeling as if life was spinning about. She didn't know how it came to be like this, but it certainly wasn't like she could really let this stop.

"Thank you dear. I'm trying my best, I swear by that," she said.

Kayla knew that the meeting she had tomorrow would determine a few things. It was a meeting that her father called regarding what she was doing. He was always trying to buy her out, and she didn't know how much of this she could take.

It was such a messy situation, but for now, she couldn't worry Amelia about it.

"You sure you're okay?" Amelia asked.

"Yes, I swear by it. Don't you worry," Kayla explained.

Amelia nodded, feeling a flush ghost against her cheeks.

"Good. I do care about you a lot, which is definitely a big thing for me too," Amelia stated. Kayla could see the serious look in her face, which screamed of concern.

She was happy Amelia was worried, but she didn't want Amelia to worry on her behalf. It wasn't right.

"I'll be okay. Trust me," Kayla said.

It was a sort of mantra for herself more than anything. She honestly was a little worried about the meeting. Her father sent her a text message despite her insistence that she didn't want to be bothered. It pissed her off more than anything else though simply because her dad didn't seem to give a flying fuck about her own well-being.

That night though, Kayla needed to stay strong for Amelia. She needed to prove to Amelia that this was definitely okay. After they cuddled for a bit, having sex once again, Kayla went to bed, feeling like even if shit did hit the fan tomorrow, at least she had someone there for her.

When Kayla got to the club that morning after dropping Amelia off, she pressed the voicemail system. A couple of general messages played, and then of course, one from her favorite corporation.

"Hey Kayla, this is Ted from ReidCorp. We wanted to make sure you're still on for eleven today to discuss business. We wanted to see if you thought at all about the proposal that Dave gave to you. Thanks!"

It was always like this. Kayla just wished her father, "Dave" could take the fucking hint. But of course, at eleven on the dot, a man walked in wearing a pressed black business suit. He looked around, cringing his nose, and then he looked at Kayla.

"Kayla," he simply stated.

"Cut the bullshit, Dave. I know what you're here for," Kayla snapped back. She didn't care if this man gave her half her DNA, she didn't want anything to do with him.

"I'm just here to talk. I know that Ted sent over the information about the possibility of acquisition," he said.

Kayla looked about, seeing a couple of people there looking at her.

"Come to my office. I don't discuss business matters out in the open like this," she muttered. It wasn't just that, she didn't want people getting worried about what might happen to this establishment. But of course, she knew that her own father didn't seem to care about that. But he walked inside, and immediately after, Kayla closed the door. She didn't lock it in the event she would have to get out of there.

She sat down, and, of course, her father stared at her with the look of a businessman. He didn't give off the vibe of coming for a chat.

He wanted something bigger.

"So, have you thought about the proposal that I offered to you Kayla," he said.

Kayla scoffed.

"Yeah, and I am here to tell you to shove it up your goddamn ass."

There was silence, and her father looked at her with a frown.

"Come on Kayla, I will buy this off you and we'll refurbish it into a yacht club or something. We'll pay handsomely. You know the sum that I'm offering" he said.

Kayla tensed. She damn well did, and that didn't matter a thing to her.

"Yes, and I already told you that I have zero desire to get into that with you. You're my father, and you're also a greedy, seedy businessman. I know what you've done in the past dad, and I have zero desire to be a part of it," Kayla explained.

There was a sigh, and Kayla could practically tell that her father was upset about all of this.

"Kayla, why are you so against this? I'm offering more money than you'd ever make at any other place," he said.

Kayla tensed, and she then spoke.

"It's because I don't have the desire to get into a partnership with you dad. I escaped you a few times in the past, I don't want to deal with your shit again. There's a reason I've avoided you like the plague," she said.

"Indeed. I've tried to repair our friendship there Kayla. I wish you could see things my way," he purred.

"And I wish you could fuck off! You're an abusive son of a bitch who doesn't care about anyone but himself. The only reason you're here right now is because you took the money that Mom made when she died! You took what I had and used it for yourself," Kayla spat.

The silence in the room was deafening. Her father looked at her with a cocked face.

"I thought that was all behind us. I didn't do a damn thing to—"

"Yes. You. Did. I know what you did Dave! You're not my father. You're a rat bastard who stole from me, and from your late wife. You also killed her. and now, you're trying to get rid of me. Well guess what? I'm not dealing with any of it!" she stated.

The way he looked at her made Kayla's hairs stand on end. She didn't know if standing up to her own father was the right thing to do. But then, he sighed.

"One day you'll get it Kayla. I'm not sure when, but one day, you'll get it. By the way, I heard from a friend there is a new girl here?" he asked.

Kayla paused, looking at her dad. Why did he care about Amelia?

"It's none of your damn business," she said.

"Oh, but it will be. Kayla, I highly recommend you get yourself some protection, because I want this establishment. I have the money to pay for it, and we could just go our merry way. I have the place, and you can go off and live your own life. We could make this easy," he said.

She wanted to spit in his face, but she held back. Kayla needed to keep that air of professionalism, even it meant she was practically throwing up in her goddamn mouth the moment he spoke.

"I think it's best if you get out of my face. And stay the hell away from anyone in the club. I'll find a way to get rid of you once and for all if you continue this. I'm running this club now. I'm not the girl you always knew. I'm not the one you could take advantage of, and I'm certainly not backing down without a goddamn fight dad. Or should I say Dave, because I can't even begin to fathom why such a deplorable man would even have a child. You're a monster," she said.

There was a look, and then, Kayla saw a frightening smile on his face it made her hairs stand on end, and when she looked at him, she could tell he found some sort of joy in all of this.

"My dear Kayla. I hope that one day, you see what I mean by what I do," he said.

She glared at him, disgusted by the actions, and then, shortly after, he got up, leaving the office. When she heard the door close, Kayla wanted to scream.

How could her own dad be like this? He was a disgusting human, and Kayla knew that the reason why did all of this was because she wouldn't sit there and take it sitting down. She was tired of always being hurt by this man just because he sired her.

"That fucking bastard," Kayla said.

It was always like this, but he seemed to almost hit her where it hurt far more than he did in the past. There was something almost disgusting about the way he treated her, which made her physically cringe.

For now, she had to keep her profile low, and work on trying to keep the club as nice as possible.

When she got out there, Kayla noticed Amelia speaking to a man. She said some words, and then, she noticed the man lean in. he whispered something in her ear, which caused her to put her arms up, pushing him away.

When Kayla got closer, she felt her body go white. It was her dad, who was smiling at her.

"Hey there Kayla, I'm just meeting one of the new dancers here," he said.

"You can kindly fuck of with that. Get away from the girls. That's final," Kayla said.

The man glared at her, but then, he got up. As quickly as it happened, he went away.

Kayla looked over at Amelia, who seemed as pallid as a ghost.

"What's the matter?" Kayla said.

"Oh...it's just...who was that? He kept trying to hit on me," she said.

"It's nothing. Don't give that man the time of day if you ever see him again. I'm serious Amelia," Kayla said.

She didn't want her dad harassing anyone else that was around. Amelia looked ready to argue, but the serious glare on Kayla's face got her to shut the hell up. Kayla wanted to protect Amelia, and she wanted what's best for Amelia, but there was something wrong, something very wrong about her dad, and she knew that the only way to truly find out the truth behind his actions and why he did what he did, was to get to the bottom of this.

Chapter Nine

The man who stopped at Amelia felt strangely familiar, but at the same time, Amelia had never met someone like that ever. Amelia, after talking with Kayla about it, surmised that whomever that man was, he was definitely a part of something she shouldn't be dealing with.

"Well, I'm glad you stepped in when you did. Thanks for that," Amelia said.

"You're welcome. Do you promise me that you'll stay safe though? And away from trouble?" Kayla asked.

Amelia nodded, at least to the level of trouble that was worrisome. For some reason, he gave off the vibe that he had ulterior motives, but Amelia couldn't pinpoint them.

But of course, Amelia wasn't here to deal with that. She had to get to work.

"Don't worry about me Kayla. I'm going to take care of everything later. For now, let's just get on with things, she said.

Kayla nodded, and Amelia went to work. She started serving drinks to some of the patrons, but she couldn't help but feel like she was being watched. There was something ominous about all of this, and Amelia didn't like this one bit.

Maybe it was her own personal worry about everything. It wasn't like she was alone in this either. She did have Kayla, and she felt safe and secure with Kayla around.

But there was something lurking about here which made Amelia feel nervous, and it made her realize indeed that, with everything going on, it definitely wouldn't be easy for them.

For the rest of the shift, Amelia continued working on getting drinks together. She made decent money, but as she was leaving, she opened the door. A guy that looked familiar immediately showed up, causing Amelia to tense.

"Cody?" she said.

Cody looked at her with a surprised glance. This was the guy from college who worked with her in chem class. She remembered that he was kind of a flirt, and he was always hitting on her.

This could be bad. It could be really bad.

She looked at Cody for a moment, trying her hardest to hold back, when finally, he spoke.

"Wow! I didn't expect you, of all people, to be here Amelia. I just came in to get a drink while waiting for my ride home from work but, uh, nice," he said.

Amelia flushed, but then, as quickly as it happened, she felt a presence behind her. She looked, and of course, there was Kayla. She looked at both of them with a bit of surprise on her face.

"Who is this?" she asked.

"Oh, this is Cody. He's from my classes," Amelia explained.

"I see. Hello there. I think Amelia is off the clock, so please get going," Kayla said.

Cody scoffed, looking at Kayla with a glare. Amelia hoped nothing bad would come from this. She could practically taste the glare that Kayla gave her.

"Sorry, I didn't know I was intruding on anything," he said.

He walked off, and Amelia looked at Kayla with confusion.

"What was all that for?" she asked.

"I could tell he was trying to hide something. You better be careful there Amelia. Trust me, don't get involved with guys like that," Kayla stated.

Amelia felt a little bit shocked that Kayla would say something like that. She felt like Kayla was just trying to stir trouble or something.

"You're not the boss of me Kayla. I just saw him and thought I'd say hi," she said.

"I see. Well, just be careful Amelia. I know how people can be here. I'm also a bit on edge cause of the whole mess with Dave earlier," Kayla said.

Amelia looked at Kayla with a bit of concern.

"Care to explain what that was about by the way? You looked really pressed when he was bothering you. I know it's none of my business, but...if you need anything, please talk to me," she said.

Kayla hesitated, and Amelia could tell whatever was eating at Kayla wasn't something she could easily discuss.

"It's nothing Amelia. Trust me. Now, get home. I've got it here," Kayla insisted.

Amelia didn't like that Kayla was being so avoiding about whatever was going on in her life. But, at the same time, that was typical Kayla. She always seemed to have that vibe that she didn't really want to get people involved in whatever was going on. In a strange way, it made sense, but she didn't know why Kayla was hiding the truth.

Amelia didn't get into it. For now, she had to head on home. She knew that if she was late again, her mom may ask questions.

And that was something Amelia didn't want.

When she left, she felt a strange chill in the air. She didn't know what it was. Suddenly, her phone rang. Amelia picked it up. It was her mom.

"Hey Mom, what's the matter?" Amelia asked.

"Hey, so I'm going to be home late. I just wanted to let you know. I know that usually I'm home way before you get back, but...I wouldn't mind if you took care of yourself tonight. I'm not sure how late I'll be, but I wanted to give you a bit of a heads up on it all," she said.

Amelia paused. This was the third night this way that her mom did this.

"Are you sure you're okay, Mom? You're usually never gone like this," Amelia said.

There was another long pause. What was her mother hiding? Finally, her mother spoke, and Amelia felt slightly hurt by it.

"It's nothing Amelia. Trust me on this. Now, get going. I'll be back late tonight. And how is work going by the way? You seem to be doing decently given all the time you spend out there," she said.

Amelia didn't know how to tell her mom that this was the best damn job that she had in a long time. For now, she was just going to pretend that all she did was serve customers alcohol. Although that was a total lie, she definitely didn't want to get into the logistics of it.

Well, she did serve alcohol, but not at some innocuous club. If she knew the truth, things would get bad.

"All right. Be safe. I love you," her mom said.

"Love you too, Mom," Amelia replied.

The phone clicked off, and Amelia sighed. She didn't know why talking with her mom made her feel so on edge. Was it because her mom had a bad habit of seemingly knowing when something was up? Or was it the fact that she was always asking so many questions, when she would keep her own life hidden from Amelia in most cases? Whatever the case, Amelia didn't want to deal with the fallout from that.

Tonight, she'd be walking home alone anyway. It was a normal thing for her but tonight something felt off.

It felt different and it felt like Amelia was definitely not just here on her own terms. She tried to shake the feeling of getting the hell out of there and hiding away. But, when she walked past the third block, before the busy intersection, she felt someone creeping behind her.

Who was it? Who could it be? Did Kayla come out for some reason? Was Cody following her? No, Kayla would stop that right away the moment she saw it. Whoever was following her didn't feel right, and she didn't like the way this felt.

Maybe it was just her own imagination. Maybe it was just her own fears. But then, as she was about to turn around, someone grabbed her arms.

She tried to fight it. She tried to get past them, and then, she felt something forced to her face. What the hell was going on?

She tried to fight this, breathing out and trying her best to keep herself together. But the hand was right up against her face now, holding it there as she tried to cry out. Then, she relaxed, feeling as if her entire body lost all its energy. Before she could say anything else, she fell to the ground.

"Good. This will get her to listen to me," the voice said.

It was a familiar one, but Amelia didn't recognize it. She was unconscious, a victim of the madness that this bastard had planned.

Chapter Ten

Kayla felt off.

She couldn't pinpoint where it came from. Who was making her feel this way? She tried to text Amelia, who normally answered right away, but the was no response.

"What the hell is going on?" she asked herself.

She couldn't believe that this was happening. She didn't know why she let Amelia leave on her own. Something felt so off, so weird about all of this, and it made her feel like she had to find Amelia right away.

What happened to cause this though? Kayla felt fine earlier. Was it because of her dad? Or was it that guy who came in.

Cody.

He sat around like it was nothing. And when Kayla walked over toward him, he put his hand up.

"What's the matter?" Kayla said, trying to sound friendly, but looking over this man because she didn't know what to make of him. Was he a friend? Or was he trying to do something else.

"Hey. So, I'm sorry if I did anything to piss you off. Amelia is a sweet woman. She's never shown interest in me, but I do like her and—"

"She's not straight," Kayla simply said.

The guy looked at Kayla with shock on his face.

"Wait, seriously? I just thought she was too nervous to admit that she liked someone," he said.

Kayla wanted to smack this guy upside the head. Where did he get the idea that Amelia was straight? Was he a special kind of stupid or something?

"Where did you get that idea?" Kayla said.

"I don't know. I've always thought she was cute, and I thought she just didn't want a boyfriend or anything," he said.

Kayla laughed.

"Nah, she's got a girlfriend. But, I am worried about her. she's with someone who has her own set of baggage, and a whole lot of crap," Kayla said.

The guy looked at Kayla, and then, he nodded.

"Yeah, I feel that. I know that her mom is kind of a hardass too. I was shocked to see her working here of all places. I'm pretty sure her mom is not supposed to know that," he said.

"Yeah, and if anyone says anything, I'm going to make sure they don't say anything again," Kayla said.

The other guy looked affronted but then nodded.

"Fair enough. Thanks though. You seem cool," Cody said.

"I try to be. I know how things can be here," Kayla said.

"Yeah. There's just…something off about coming here. I was meeting with a guy for a job, and then, someone came over and tried to ask me about Amelia. He said his name was Dave. He told me he had business with her, but I don't know how he knows her? It was just strange," he said.

At that moment, Kayla practically dropped everything.

"I'm sorry, I need to go," she said.

"Are you sure? What about—"

Kayla stepped back.

"enjoy your time here. I need to take care of a few things outside," she said.

Kayla raced over to the phones, dialing for Mandy. After two rings, Mandy picked up.

"Hey, what's the matter?" she asked.

"Emergency. I need you to watch the club. I think one of my dancers is getting stalked right now, so I need to go check on her," Kayla explained.

"Oh crap! I'll be there in a second," she said.

The phone clicked off, and Kayla started to feel a shakiness. She didn't know where in the world Amelia was. That was why she wasn't answering her damn phone.

She knew who took her, the reasoning behind it. Kayla knew for a fact that...if things did get bad, she would need to take care of her past. It would mean blood on her hands, but she didn't care.

She opened the secret compartment in the bottom drawer of her desk. After fishing around, she pulled out something from the back.

A gun.

It was a mini mm. she kept it around in case if the club ever got attacked. She just thought she'd never have to use it on her own father. She looked at the machine, and she checked for ammo.

Six bullets.

That's all she had.

Kayla packed the gun in her holster that she wore under her jacket. As soon as she did, she heard the door open, and Mandy come in.

"There you are? Is everything okay?" she said.

"No. it seems Dave has his own agenda," Kayla said.

"I see. He's still causing trouble, is he?" Mandy said.

"Yeah, with my girlfriend. Listen Mandy, if I don't make it...the club is in your hands. I need to go protect Amelia from...this," she said.

Mandy nodded.

"I see. Well, good luck. I believe in you," she said.

"Thanks, but I don't need luck. I need to give my father a goddamn piece of my mind," Kayla said.

She raced on out of there, grabbing her phone and punching the number for her father's office in. it went straight to voicemail, but she did have his cell number. After a couple of rings, she heard her father speak.

"Hello there Kayla," he said.

"Cut the crap Dave. Where the hell is Amelia?" she asked.

"Oh, she's right here with me. A little knocked out right now, but she's safe and sound. I can assure you that I'm taking proper care of her, and she'll be kept safe and sound until the demands are over," he said.

Kayla tensed. She knew that this was dangerous. If things went bad...she could die.

But this was a risk she was willing to take. She knew that her life wasn't easy, that she was a bad girl, and she would do whatever it took to protect Amelia at all costs.

"Leave her alone, and don't you dare touch her."

Chapter Eleven

Amelia started coming to, looking around at the space. It was an office, and there was an oaken desk nearby, and that man from earlier sitting there.

Dave.

He was looking forward, tapping the pen he had on his fingers there, and soon, he looked over at Amelia, smiling.

"There you are cutie. I'm surprised it took you this long to wake up," he said.

Amelia tensed. She didn't like the way this man was looking at her. it made her feel uncomfortable, and it made her realize that she was indeed a bit off about it all.

"What...what's going on?" she asked.

"Simple. I'm waiting for your girlfriend to come over. My daughter," he said.

Kayla was his daughter? What the hell was this? She looked at him, and then at his desk. He had a series of papers there, strewn all over.

"What are you doing here though? Why are you doing this?" she asked.

"Simple. I want what's mine," he said.

"But...this isn't yours," she said.

"It can be if I get the right asking price for it. My daughter has caused nothing but trouble for me. It's a family affair, but you're used as collateral. She won't listen to me unless I give her a...bargaining chip. And you of course, are the bargaining chip that will certainly make a whole bunch of splashes," he said to Amelia.

Amelia tried to move, but her hands were tied together. The same went for her feet. She didn't understand. What the heck kind of family situation was this? She didn't even know anymore, and that was the scariest part of all of this.

"Why do you do this? Why now?" she asked.

"Because...she owes me this. She built this because of me," he said.

Amelia didn't believe that in the very least. It sounded so farfetched that even she felt like something was off.

"You're lying," she said.

"I'm not. Trust me on this," he said.

There was a long pause, and Amelia couldn't help but feel like something was very wrong. She started to look over at the other man, and she knew that there was something downright evil about him.

"You want to make her life miserable? But why?" Amelia asked.

"Simple. She didn't stay when she should have. I planned to provide all for her. I'm the one who was going to take care of her for the rest of her life, the one to help her throughout her days, and of course, this stupid bitch just throws it all away," he said in response.

Amelia was disgusted by it all. She didn't know why, but something about this felt so wrong, so weird, and she couldn't help but feel like there was definitely something amiss here.

"Fuck off," she said, spitting at him.

He came over, brandishing a knife, bringing it toward Amelia's face.

"What was that? You want to talk like that again?" he said.

This man was just as crazy as Amelia expected him to be. Maybe that's because Kayla was so adamant about not talking about this. She felt afraid. She felt fear for the first time in a long time. There was something almost terrifying about it all.

It made her feel ill at ease, that's for sure. She started to look at him, and then, he pulled back.

"No, I need you alive. For now," he said.

For now. Those words made Amelia's hairs stand on end. It felt so wrong, so weird to her, and she wanted nothing more than to just disappear into the horizon or something forever.

After what felt like forever, she noticed her dad sit down again, lighting up a cigar and smoking.

"It's perfect payment. She'll give the club over to me, and then I'll turn it into something worthwhile. I'll make sure that it's everything that she couldn't do. She'll pay for her insolence," he said.

Amelia felt like everything he was saying was just contrived words. Something about this felt so off, like he was hiding the entire truth from her. There was nary another look around though, and Amelia didn't want to get threatened again. Something had to give though, and she feared the worst.

After a little bit, there was the sound of the door opening, and soon, Amelia wondered if she was really here, if Kayla really came to save her. she hoped so.

She didn't want to be here for any longer than she was already. This place feels stuffy, gross, and the way her father looked at her made Amelia feel like she was in the spotlight.

"So, are you just a fuck buddy? A friend? Or are you her girlfriend?" he asked Amelia.

Was he talking about her relationship with Kayla? She didn't even know anymore. Something about this just felt so off. She felt like no matter what, she would end up getting some crap from this.

"I don't need to tell you any of that," she said.

"What was that?" he asked, walking toward her.

She hesitated once again. Was he actually going to hurt her? She didn't want to believe so, but there was a part of her that felt slightly frightened by the situation. It felt so off, there was something so weird about all of this. But then, as he was about to threaten her again, the door started to open.

Amelia tensed, hesitating right then and there. What was about to happen here? What would go on now? She honestly didn't even know anymore. Something about this felt so off, so different from the normal life that she was used to, that for now, she just sat there, watching with shock in her eyes that this was happening. After that, she noticed the door swing open, her heart racing. A feeling of relief rushed through her body as she heard the next few words.

"You'll pay for this, Dad."

Chapter Twelve

Kayla rushed in, preparing her next attack. Amelia looked up at her, smiling in excitement.

"You're here!" she said.

"Course I am. I'm here to stop this bastard from harassing my girlfriend," Kayla said.

She couldn't believe her father. Kidnapping her daughter's girlfriend and harassing her like this. It made Kayla sick to her stomach. She didn't know what she would do right now, but she had one plan, and one plan only.

And that of course, was to fight back.

But her dad sat there, patting the area across from her.

"Come on Kayla, I just want to talk. It put things into a little bit more of a...perspective," he said.

Kayla hesitated.

She had her gun in her hand, hiding it of course. What did he want? She then looked at him and sat down gingerly across.

"What do you want dad? Or should I say Dave, because what kind of sick bastard does this to their kid," she said.

"Oh, I'm just here to give you some encouragement Kayla. Trust me, you seem to like it," he said.

Kayla paused, looking at her dad. What was his endgame? What did he plan to do with everything here?

"What do you want with me, Dad? Why do you keep doing this?" she asked.

"Isn't it obvious there Kayla? I want what's mine," he said.

What as his? She looked at him with concern and confusion.

"What do you mean? None of this is yours whatsoever, so what does that mean?" she asked.

"It's simple, really. I want you to give me what's mine. The business," he said lowly.

Kayla paused.

"It isn't yours. I made this on my own. I got my own loan out, paid it back, and I grew it to where it is today. You're just bullying me because you believe this is the right thing to do," she said.

He looked at her, shaking his head.

"You seriously think that? No, I made sure that they gave the loan, so that you could be approved for it," he replied. T

That sounded like a bunch of bullshit. It didn't seem right, and for Amelia, something about this sounded off. She looked at him with a glare, and then, after a brief second, she spoke.

"You're lying. I know that you are. I know the truth about you father. You literally run a syndicate of men who want nothing more than to control everything. And the thing is, I'm not here for that. In fact, I'm not going to be the one who finishes you off either," she stated.

He looked at her with both concern, and curiosity.

"Really now? And why do you say that? Don't you want your revenge? Your time to take me out and all," he teased.

"I'd love that dad, but I think…I think I'm going to let these guys do it," Kayla said.

Suddenly, the door busted open, and a bunch of officers came in. Kayla's father stood up, looking at Kayla with a glance.

"Die you little bitch!" he said.

He pulled out a gun, and then, there was a bang. Kayla narrowly escaped it, but of course, the police officers were at her father, taking him down instantly. For a long time, her father didn't move, and when they arrested him, they looked at Kayla, nodding.

"Take him away. Obviously, this bastard has a laundry list of crap," she said.

The men agreed, nodding as they pulled him out of there. When the door finally closed, they were alone in the office.

"What now?" Amelia said.

"I ordered the team to take my dad downtown. They traced the conversation we had, and it turns out my dad was avoiding a lot. But, that's a whole other problem for a whole other day, so let's get this all settled right now. I think you deserve an explanation," Kayla said.

She didn't like being forced to explain herself, but she could see the fear in Amelia's eyes. She felt guilty that she didn't tell Amelia sooner, and as she finished up with the last of the ropes, she pulled Amelia into her arms. Amelia and she hugged for a long time, both of them holding one another for a brief second. For a long time, neither of them moved, both of them happy to have one another in this moment.

"Should we go check on your dad?" Amelia asked.

"Nah. Cops would call me and brief me on the situation after they talked with him. But there is one last thing that I do need to do before we get out of here., I think explaining all of this over coffee or some food is probably good. You're not hurt though, right?" Kayla asked.

Amelia shook her head.

"No. just a little shaken up," she said.

"It's all right. I learned how to fight someone like that a long time ago, back when I first opened the club. I've been in my fair share of scrapes, but I didn't expect my own dad to pull a gun on me," Kayla said with a laugh.

"Well, I guess some people are surprising then," Amelia said.

"Damn right. But before we go, I want to take care of what's on the table," Kayla said.

She walked over to the document, pulling it up and looking at it. It's a document that says that the rights to the business would be given to Dave. Kayla grabbed the lighter in her pocket, holding it there, and then burning the contents. She did that with the rest of the documents and then, she went to her dad's computer.

"Let me take care of one last thing," she said.

Amelia watched with surprise as Kayla typed in a few things. She then saw that there was a series of files about this whole transaction, all of which included fabricated statements and comments.

"Of course," she said, pursing her lips as she looked at it.

Her dad was notorious for this, and it pissed her off. She then went to each file, mass deleting them so that they ended up falling into the abyss. Amelia stood there, watching the whole debacle in place.

"Everything...better now?" she asked.

"As good as it can be Amelia. Trust me, it's not ideal, but I definitely am a bit worried. I don't feel like he' coming back, but I had to be on the safe side, you know," Kayla explained.

She didn't think her dad had much left in him. He messed up, and he lost. She was the winner in this fight. But still, there was something almost unsettling about all of this which made Kayla realize that this wasn't just the end of a time, but also the beginning of something more.

She looked over at Amelia, who deserved and applanation. She needed it, especially since her own father was such a douchebag, and randomly did that to her.

It disgusted Kayla what he did to Amelia. Her girlfriend, maybe someone more, shouldn't be at the mercy of a man's actions like that.

It was definitely time.

After Kayla finished deleting most of that information and moving the other stuff to a file for the police, she closed the computer, turning to Amelia.

"Let's go get some food," she said.

"How did you get rid of that? How did you get into the computer? Did you...know or something?" Amelia asked.

"Yeah. My dad is an asshole, but he's also an idiot who doesn't change his passwords. So, it was one of the three passwords he had," she admitted.

"I see," Amelia said.

"Anyway, let's get the hell out of here I hate staying in this goddamn place," she said.

Amelia agreed to that. As they were leaving though, Kayla stopped, grabbing Amelia's hand and pulling it over. She looked at her, and for a long time, neither of them said anything. Then, Kayla spoke.

"Listen, I'm really happy that you weren't hurt or anything," she said.

"Thank you Kayla. I am too. I was worried about that as well," Amelia said.

Kayla gave her a long, passionate kiss ad for a long time, neither wanted to move. They felt like if they did, the dream would go away. Kayla still couldn't believe that her father, one of the most abusive men from her past, was finally put away, and that the police would do something about it.

She knew that he was just a symptom of the world out there. The greedy cats, the bastards who wanted nothing more than to destroy the fabric of society that was left. But Amelia was here, and Kayla was safe for now. Even if things did go bad, she felt that once things got better, they'd be happier.

They left with their hands in one another's, and for Kayla, she wanted to protect Amelia, to have her by her side, and to be near her, no matter what.

Chapter Thirteen

For Amelia, it was all a whirlwind. She knew that Kayla had an interesting past, but she didn't expect that sort of thing. When they got to the diner down the street, the server sat them both down, taking drink orders for two coffees, and two burgers.

The place was both quiet, but also busy enough where an intimate conversation like this could be had. For Amelia, she was just happy to be alive right about now.

"How are you feeling?" Kayla asked.

"As good as I can be. What about you?"

"I've been better," Kayla retorted with a smile on her face.

"Yeah, I figured whatever happened with your dad was something you're not comfy talking about then, right?" Amelia asked.

"No, I am. See, the thing is Amelia, my dad is an asshole. He doesn't care about anyone but himself. Ever since I was a kid, he...he's been like this. But it was in a different way," Kayla explained.

Amelia looked at her with surprise on her face, unsure what to say.

"How so?" she inquired.

"Well, for starters I honestly am surprised he sobered up enough to get to where he is today. For most of my childhood he was a raging alcoholic. That is...until my mom started getting sick," she said.

Amelia listened to Kayla's words, surprised by everything at hand. What did she mean? How did her mom get sick?"

"What happened? If you don't mind me asking?" Amelia questioned.

There was a paused and then, Kayla sighed.

"It's a bit of a long story but my dad did kill my mom. It was a bit inadvertent, at least that's what he claims, but I don't think it was. I think he did this on purpose," Kayla explained.

"How so?" Amelia replied. She had a bad feeling about this.

"For starters, I never said it to anyone m but II found a syringe next to my mom while she was dying in the hospital. I didn't think it belonged to any of the doctors, so I never told anyone. But they did find it later on, and confirmed it wasn't supposed to be there. They questioned me since I was one of the many people to spend time with her. I told them I had no idea how in the world it happened, and after some serious interrogation, they finally let me go. But, my dad however...they never questioned him. I found out my dad had a company that afforded enough money to pay off those bastards, so he was able to walk away like it was nothing. I'm shocked honestly. My dad was hiding a secret business from me, and he couldn't even pay for mom's hospital bills. He told me that if she did come out, we'd have to pay them together. I told him I was in school, it wasn't fair. But, he didn't care. She cared more about saving face and being able to sit there and act like nothing was wrong than to help his daughter. It sickened me, I'm going to admit," Kayla said.

Amelia reached out, touching Amelia's shoulder. Amelia leaned in, sighing in frustration.

"I'm sorry for putting all of this on you Amelia. It's just...hard to talk about. I never did, and it wasn't easy for me to come forward with everything at hand," she said.

"I know. But you're so brave, and you've done so much. You're certainly something," Amelia replied.

She wished she was at least half as strong as Kayla was.

"That's not the end of the story though. This all happened right before my first semester. Her dying, and my dad acting fishy. After she passed I...I had a huge fight with my dad. The two of us were shouting at one another, screaming insults at one another, different things that I never really said to him up till now. We were always fighting together, and it was pretty damn terrible. But, after a bit, we both agreed that something had to give. He told me either I would have to leave college and get a job, or I'd be kicked out of the house with zero support. I told him to go fuck himself and left on my own terms. But the problem is, when I left, that's when the financial aid mysteriously stopped," Kayla explained.

Amelia leaned in, listening to her.

"What do you mean?"

"I said what I said. Somehow, all of the financial aid I was supposed to get from this was long gone, and it...it wasn't fun at all. I hated it. I lost all my support, was out on the streets for the most part. I spent a chunk of my time couch surfing, until one day the people I was staying with said I needed to do something," Kayla replied.

Amelia listened, but then, as Kayla was about to tell the next part of the story that she had.

"Well, I decided on a whim that I would open a club. I tried to look for some of the options that we had. Most of the clubs in the area were all right, but there wasn't a strip club. So, I decided to open one up. I figured putting it in this part of town will definitely help the area. And sure enough, it changed the space. At first, this area was pretty bad, and so many people struggled with coming in. there was crime, but over time, as the club got more popular, that riffraff started to leave. I changed the place, cleaned it up, and I was able to build the world that I have now," Kayla told Amelia.

"Wow. That's amazing," Amelia said.

"Yeah. I feel like a different person because of all of this. I feel like, I changed the fate of the world in my own way. I was happier. I did so much more because of this decision, and I didn't want it to end. I soon became the stirp club owner I wanted to," Kayla replied.

Amelia was pretty amazed by all of this. She knew that life wasn't easy for Kayla, and the fact that she was being so honest about it, so transparent about the way things were, was something which made Amelia happy.

"Thank you," Amelia said.

"For what"

"For...being there for me. I'm just so happy you still are, despite it all. I know this isn't easy for us, but we'll make it," Amelia said.

Kayla had a lot going on, but for Amelia, it meant that they could be together no matter what if they did keep this going, this energy that they shared together.

It felt so different, such a different vibe than what Amelia was used to. And yet, she was happy about all of that.

After a bit, Kayla sighed, and Amelia looked at her with concern. Kayla then took a deep breath, looking at Amelia with a serious glance.

"Listen, Amelia, I know that it's not easy to hear this. My dad abused me far more than I care to admit. He's done some pretty unspeakable things to me. But, I feel like I've won. Even with the hardship I've gone through, I'm happy. And I can't thank you enough. I really do appreciate all that you've done to help me Amelia," Kayla said.

Amelia flushed, realizing that Kayla meant everything.

"You mean this, right?"

"Yeah, I damn well do. You're amazing Amelia, and really worthwhile to me. So, thanks," Kayla said to her.

Amelia flushed, but then, she nodded. She could see that Kayla was thankful for all of this, and Amelia couldn't help but feel like everything was better now that they got their feelings out in the open like this.

"You're welcome Kayla. But there is one thing that still is bothering me. Something that I wanted to ask you," Amelia said.

"What is it?" Kayla asked.

Amelia tensed, feeling slightly embarrassed by her words. She didn't know what Kayla thought about their relationship. Did she really mean the whole girlfriend thing?"

"When you sad that I was your girlfriend, did you mean it? For real?" Amelia asked.

Kayla then paused, looking at Amelia and then nodding in response.

"Yeah. I meant that. I wanted to ask you out for a little bit, but I was afraid to ask. I didn't want to make it weird or anything," she said.

Amelia blushed, but then, she nodded.

"Thanks. I mean it too. I like you a lot Kayla, and I appreciate all that you've done for me. It's a lot, and I am glad you feel the same way about us, being girlfriends," she said.

"I do Amelia. I really do," Kayla said.

Amelia paused, and then, she looked at Kayla with a serious look on her face.

"So, there is one question I have for you. If you're willing to answer it," Amelia said.

"What's up?" Kayla asked.

"I was wondering if you'd let me dance. I thought about doing it a couple of times, but I wasn't sure if I was ready to try it. But now I want to," she said.

Amelia wondered how it would be if she did take up dancing. Would it change the way things were for the better, or would it be for the worst? She looked at Kayla, who seemed torn on this.

"You're sure about this right? Dancing and waitressing are different. I can give you both jobs. You can dance while still serving customers. Just know that I also don't have any responsibility if you do get hurt. You can't sue the club or anything. I only say that because I know there are women who do have this kind of idea in their heads, but then they end up getting hurt. I just don't want to be responsible for that," Kayla explained.

Amelia knew the risks. It was definitely something she thought about for a bit.

"Don't worry, I know my risks. I just want to dance to see how things would go. If I don't like it, I'll stay off the stage. I'm already making bank. Enough to make my mom slightly concerned," Amelia said with a smile.

"I see. Just please be safe Amelia. I don't want your mom to ask questions, and you potentially get in trouble," Kayla said.

Amelia knew that Kayla meant well.

"Listen, when I have enough money, I wouldn't mind...moving in together and whatnot. I don't want to do it right away. Not with all of the crap you'll have to deal with right now. But, down the road. If you're game, I am too," Amelia replied with a smile on her face.

Kayla paused for a moment, and Amelia hoped that she wasn't too forward. But then, Kayla smiled.

"You've got a deal," Kayla said with a grin.

Amelia felt like she was the queen of the world. She then moved in, giving Kayla a kiss on the cheek.

"Thanks. Anyway, we should probably head back. I know that my mom is probably wondering where the hell I've been," she pointed out.

Kayla nodded.

"Yeah, I have to find out from the police as well what they plan to do with my dad and everything.

Because I don't want anything to do with him right now," she said.

Kayla seemed to have meant it, and Amelia felt that feeling. She didn't like her dad either.

"Yeah, anyway, I had a good time. And...thanks for being honest Kayla. I appreciate all that you've told me," Amelia replied.

Kayla blushed, but then she responded, and Amelia could practically feel the heat on Kayla's face.

"The feeling is mutual Amelia. I'm just...glad that we could talk about this. That's all," she said.

"You and me both," Amelia said with a laugh.

They parted ways after they hugged and kissed goodbye, insisting that they'd see one another in a few more days. When Amelia got home though, she noticed that her mom was sitting at the dining room table, eating food.

"You're late," she said.

"Sorry Mom, I had to see someone. A friend. Lots of things...happened, that's all," Amelia said.

"I see. Well, is there anything you feel you need to tell me?" she asked.

Amelia paused, but then shook her head.

"None in particular. I'm going to head to my room though. I've got another long day tomorrow," Amelia replied.

As she headed upstairs, her mother spoke.

"By the way, I'll be gone next Saturday to see someone. I would rather you not throw parties here, but if you do want to let anyone stay over, that's fine," she said.

Amelia nodded.

"I'll think about that," she said.

Amelia made her way to her room, sitting down at the computer. She wondered just how much her mom knew.

Hopefully, not enough to get her in trouble, but Amelia had no idea. She didn't know how her mom acted, and the way she ran things anymore. She got an email from Kayla saying that this was the form for stripping. Amelia filled it out. It was your typical waiver, where nobody would be held responsible at the club for her actions.

Amelia just wanted to try it. She felt that it was a form of expression, and this was something that she wanted to try. When she finally finished, she pressed send, sitting down and holding herself back.

Things were about to change. She didn't know how much her mom knew, but she planned to keep her in the dark for as long as she could.

That was the only way to make things right, but little did she know that her mom would find out sooner rather than later, and when she did, both Amelia ad Kayla would have a choice.

Chapter Fourteen

When Kayla got in the car, she opened up her phone, calling the police station. They called her back in the middle of dinner, but Kayla didn't want to take it. But, now was as good of a time as ever to find out what they planned to do with her asshole of a father.

"Hello?" the person on the other end said.

"Hey, this is Kayla. Dave's daughter. I...I wanted to find out what the verdict was on him, and what they were going to do with him. I know that they were planning on indicting him, but I wanted to hear from you directly," she said.

There was a pause, and then, shortly after, the other voice spoke.

"Well, we've made a few decisions on this. Your father tried very hard to get out of this, but he won't be able to. We decided to arrest him and address the charges at hand. He's got a long track record Kayla. If you do want to see him, now is the time," the officer said.

Kayla had no desire to see the rat bastard, but there was still something which bothered her.

"No thanks, I'd rather not. But there is one thing which I'd like to have the answer to."

There was a long pause, and then, the other officer on the end spoke.

"What is it?"

"His business. Who's going to take care of it?" Kayla asked. She wondered if it would be given to her on a whim. She didn't want it, but maybe selling it for a profit would be decent.

There was yet another pause, and Kayla expected the officer to be bringing out some long, legal papers explaining how her dad would keep it somehow. But instead the words that he said definitely were quite surprising.

"We found out that he will not be able to sell that business. He actually already sold it to another investor and is trying very desperately at the moment to get this back. But, for now, he's not going to be able to hold onto that. For now, he's not able to do anything besides wait for the official verdict from the jury. But we expect for it to be a long sentence, and one he won't be able to be released early on," he said.

Kayla felt a feeling of both annoyance, and relief. She wanted to take that property off his hands, but the fact that it was already in the hands of another investor wasn't necessarily a bad thing.

"Thank you. I'm glad that he won't be getting out anytime soon. It's...it's something that makes me happy in its own way," Kayla said.

"The feeling is mutual. We are glad to have helped in our own way. Take care of yourself," he said.

The phone clicked off, and when Kayla heard all this, she felt a feeling of freedom. She never had to worry about whether or not people would come to the club. She did some digging, and of course the new investor was focused on just that company and had zero desire in acquiring other assets at this point in time. In a strange way, that was the most relieving part of all of this, and Kayla was here for it all.

Despite all that happened, Kayla was finally free. Now, she could work on her relationship with Amelia, which mattered more to her. Amelia sent her a text telling her that she filled out the form, but there was another part of the message which surprised Kayla.

By the way, my mom is not going to be around for a little bit this Saturday. Care to hang out?

Kayla wondered if that was the right idea, but there was something exciting about that. She was definitely yearning for a bit of freedom at this point, a reward for all of the garbage she had to deal with up till now.

Kayla quickly responded, saying that she would love to spend some time with Amelia. It might've come off as a little bit desperate, but the fact that Kayla could live her own life at this point without someone here made her feel happy as well.

The next few days felt like a whirlwind. Kayla had a couple of pieces of paper from the police department, basically signing her as the person who would get the assets that her own father didn't even bother to leave for her, but they didn't go to anyone else. Kayla took them and sold them, not giving a damn about any of that crap.

Kayla was just happy that she could have this normal sort of life, and the way life was definitely made her happy as well.

It was a new life, a new future for both of them, one that made them both happier than ever. Amelia seemed to be doing well with the whole dancing thing.

Kayla started her off with a couple of days of it, and soon, she let Amelia move onto doing it whenever she wanted to. At first, Kayla insisted that she just stay on the stage, but then, after a couple of weeks, Amelia was able to work on using the pole for basic tricks.

"I'm doing it! This is so fun," she said.

Kayla couldn't help but admire Amelia's body. She had a gorgeous body, and it looked even better on stage too. Amelia seemed to know exactly how to strut her stuff, moving about, and she started to move her hips in a way that was simple, yet tantalizing.

It was like watching a whole new world whenever Amelia went on stage.

Kayla thought it was the most attractive thing, and of course, the other people watching Amelia's set thought the same. Kayla would look at some of the other people who were here, watching Amelia dance and move her hips on stage. It was so amazing to them, and for Kayla, she couldn't help but feel like this was a whole treat for her as well. After a little bit, Kayla and Amelia realized that this was a great thing for both of them. Amelia became one of the top dancers at the club, making more money, and after two months, she generated revenue that even Kayla didn't expect.

The biggest challenge was of course, keeping this from Amelia's mom. Amelia's mom did begin asking questions. One day, Amelia came in, looking behind her shoulder. Kayla looked up from the paperwork she was doing, and she spoke.

"Something the matter?" she asked.

"Yeah. Sorry, I'm a little bit stressed out. My mom apparently found the grip that I had, the pole grip. She asked me why I had it. I told her it was yours, and she started questioning me on this. I'm a bit worried Kayla. I really am. I thought about possibly moving out soon. I wanted to talk to you about that, but I'm not sure how," Amelia admitted.

Kayla knew this day would come. She knew that one day, Amelia would have to come forth with the truth.

"I wanted to talk with you about that too. Let's do it after work though," she said.

Amelia nodded.

"Can I wait tables tonight? I don't feel comfy doing pole work when I'm this stressed out," she said.

Kayla nodded.

"Yeah. That's fine."

Amelia smiled giving her a passionate kiss before heading to the bar, moving her hands and preparing drinks.

For Kayla, she was worried about it all. She didn't even know anymore what to do, or even what to say. She knew that her mom would bother Amelia and her eventually. Kayla just wanted Amelia to be happy, but it certainly was proving harder and harder to do every single day.

That night, after the doors were locked, Amelia sat down at one of the tables, counting the money there.

"This is more than I've made in a long time," she said.

"I see. That's good right?"

"It's wonderful Kayla, but I'm worried my mom will find out eventually. She doesn't know I have a lot saved up already. I've been thinking of getting out of her place though, for my own mental health," Amelia said.

Kayla thought about it. Her apartment was open for another person.

"I mean, I did just kick out the last person. Well, more like they just couldn't live there anymore. There was a lot going on, and I'm alone currently. I wouldn't be against you moving in as a temporary measure, or even a permanent one," Kayla said.

Amelia blushed.

"You...you mean it?" she asked.

"Of course, I don't want you to feel discomforted in your own home. You're a good person Amelia. I don't want you to feel like you have to hide yourself. Besides, even I'm tired of you hiding and all," Kayla said.

Amelia smiled, a beaming grin.

"Thank you Kayla. I'm just...worried that's all," Amelia said.

"About ow she's going to react. Don't be. I'm sure she'll be upset, like really upset, but the thing is, you need to be able to take it upon yourself to do what's right for you. Be the person you've always wanted to be, and be the guiding force in all this," Kayla said.

Amelia nodded, smiling at Kayla with a grin.

"Thank you Kayla. For everything," Amelia said.

"You're most welcome," Kayla said.

She gave Amelia a kiss, and for a moment, the two of them stayed like that. Kayla didn't want to let her go, but she knew for a fact that she had to. Tonight, Amelia would make a stand. She would tell her mom the truth, even if it did get awkward for them.

"By the way, would you mind coming with me to my place," Amelia said.

"Right now? But what about—"

"I need you to come with me Kayla," Amelia insisted.

Helping Amelia through this felt a bit nerve-wracking to say the least. Kayla wanted to do what was best for her partner, but she felt nervous about it as well.

"All right, I'll come along with you," Kayla said.

She wondered how this would go. She could see the fire in Amelia's eyes, however. The stress of the moment, and the situation of course, was weighing heavily on both of them, and for both Kayla and Amelia, things were definitely changing.

Kayla just hoped Amelia would push through it easily.

Chapter Fifteen

Amelia felt ready.

Her mother called her earlier that day, saying that they needed to talk after she got home. She said it was important. While Amelia feared what her own mother would have to say, she also knew that with Kayla by her side, things would get easier with time.

But she did wonder what would happen now.

When they got to the house, Amelia noticed there was a second car there. Who was this guy? Amelia wondered if this was what her own mother wanted to talk with her about. If that was the case, this was about to get a whole lot more interesting.

Kayla looked at Amelia with concern as she got out.

"Are you sure you'll be okay?"

"Yeah. Just please, come with me Kayla. I need you there. My mom's been acting really weird, and I don't know why," Amelia replied.

Kayla looked like she was about to argue, but she stopped, looking at Amelia, and for a long time, they didn't say a word toward one another. Soon, they stepped to the door. Amelia unlocked it, hearing the clicking as she opened up the door.

"Mom?" she asked.

"There you are," a voice barked.

Amelia tensed up. That was definitely her mom. She walked into the doorway, closing the door. Soon, Kayla followed her, but Amelia couldn't help but feel like all eyes were on her.

This wasn't good.

Amelia felt like she was in a whole different world. She wanted to say something to her mom, but she didn't know what to say. When she got there, she saw her mom with a guy that was eerily familiar, and someone whom she never thought she'd ever see in her house.

"Cody?" Amelia said.

"Hey Amelia. How is it going?" he said.

What the hell was he doing here? She looked at her mother, who was turned away.

"Wait. He's the new guy?" Amelia barked.

"Well you see Amelia. I thought—"

Amelia couldn't believe this. Her own mother was over here, trying to hook up with younger and younger men, and Amelia was supposed to feel bad for falling for a woman.

"What the hell Mom?" she said.

"Amelia, I was about to tell you. But I found out as well you've been hiding stuff from me," her mother said.

Amelia hesitated, looking over at her own mom, trying her hardest to keep herself together.

"What the hell are you talking about? She muttered.

Her mom looked over at Kayla, a glare on her face.

"And who is this?" she said.

"I'll get to that in a moment, but what do you know, Mom?" Amelia asked.

She wanted to know how much her mom did know, and how much was kept a secret. But then, her mother sighed.

"Well, I know you haven't been working at any old club for starters," she said.

"How? I'm guessing Cody told you?" Amelia snapped, glaring at Cody.

"Well, you certainly didn't do a good job of hiding it. He told me he saw you recently and I asked where. He said it was at a strip club. I can't believe you Amelia, a strip club. Have you no dignity?" her mother barked.

Amelia couldn't believe her mother of all people was questioning her dignity. Hooking up with a guy from her college class none the less.

"I mean, I have more dignity than you. I love working there. I'm a waitress, and I do a little bit of dancing," Amelia said.

"You do," Cody exclaimed.

Amelia glared at him.

"Stay out of this. You're part of the reason this is even happening," Amelia said.

"Well enough about him. Right now, we're talking Amelia. So how long have you been a disgusting stripper?"

Amelia hear the bile from her mother's words. She didn't think she was disgusting or anything, but who knows. Maybe this was normal for her mom.

"I don't know how long have you been seeing men your daughter's age? I know Cody from college mom. He's my age. It's gross how you don't like me doing what I want in life, but then here you are, hooking up with men who are old enough to be your kid. Like what the hell?" Amelia said.

"We're in love Amelia. So, who is this bitch? Your new girlfriend or something?" her mother said.

Amelia was about to cuss out her own mother for calling Kayla a bitch, but then, Kayla stepped forward, putting her hand up, and looking at Amelia's mom.

"Yes. I am her new girlfriend. And you're being unfair to your daughter. She may do stripping, but she's happy. As for you, you have your own life. You've got to realize that we're not so different, you know," Kayla stated.

"At least I'm not a disgusting bitch like you," her mother said.

Kayla immediately stepped back, and Amelia looked at her own mother. This woman has done nothing for her recently. She's been building her own life, only for her mother to make it so that she's stuck in this situation with her.

"You don't understand, Mom. You don't. You think that it's just me being irresponsible or something. Kayla helped me. She gave me a job when nobody else did. I've known her for a while. We've been through hell and back together. So please, learn to understand," Amelia stated.

There was a pause, and Amelia wondered if this would work. Her mother seemed angry by Amelia's choices.

"This is so reckless Amelia," she said.

"Oh, and apparently you're better? You're a hypocrite, Mom. Seriously, it's not fair," she said.

"And you're always doing something to get your stupid ass in trouble. I swear, I thought you'd have learned better Amelia. But I guess not. You're nothing more than a mess of a daughter and I wish...I wish you'd just leave and get out of my life," she said.

Amelia couldn't believe her mother had the balls to say something like that.

"Oh, so I'm bad because I'm not over here trying to screw everything that moves. Where's my dad by the way, Mom? Whatever happened to him? You too busy trying to screw all these guys and be reckless, but here you are, saying I'm the reckless one for falling in love with a woman, and doing something for myself," Amelia said.

Her mother looked torn, and Amelia hated that things were like this. But then, after a little bit, she sighed.

"You just don't get it, do you?" she asked.

"Yeah, I do, Mom. I get that you don't care about anyone but yourself, that if they're not following your little mold, then you're going to hate them. It's not fair, and I hate that you're always like this," she said.

Amelia couldn't take this much more. Her mom seemed to only care about herself, and she would rather just leave than stick around here.

"You're always so adamant about doing other things other than what I want. You're an insolent fool," she said.

"And you're a bitch. Honestly, I was going to tell you that I don't have any desire to stick around here either. I can't, Mom. Not with the way you act. It's better if I just leave," Amelia spat.

Her mother looked at her with shock on her face.

"You can't leave? What about me?" she asked.

"You should've thought about that before you treated me like trash," Amelia snapped.

"Least I'm not some dirty stripper," she said with a retort.

Amelia glared at her, feeling the anger ghost through her body. She couldn't believe this, and she wanted nothing more than for this to go away. She knew that with the way things were though, it would only get worse if she stuck around here. Her mother didn't care about anyone else but herself.

The big thing for Amelia, was just leaving for her own sanity and wellness. Amelia didn't know what else to do about this at the moment, other than to just let it go, and let things travel by the wayside.

For now, there wasn't much she could say in response.

"I'm a dirty stripper, sure, but have fun being alone. You don't care about anyone but yourself. Kayla and I are working to build a better business, and right now, I don't need your negativity," Amelia said in response.

She definitely didn't need this, and she couldn't help but feel like her mother was just trying to start something.

Right now, she just wanted to leave. She headed upstairs, going to her room to pack her stuff. Luckily, there was a lot already packed. When Kayla came up to the room, she looked at her with a forlorn glance.

"Are you sure you're okay? We can try to reason with her if you want," she said.

"No sense in doing so. Trust me, my mom doesn't care about anyone but herself," Amelia replied.

The realization of that really hurt. She did love her mom in a parental way, but she was so toxic that things were definitely not good for her.

It was better to just leave it all behind. Amelia finished packing her bags, and when she did so, she looked at Kayla.

"You're fine with this, right?" Amelia said.

"Yeah. I can tell she hasn't been good to you. It's obvious that you need to get the hell out of here," Kayla replied.

Amelia did agree on that. She knew staying with her toxic family would only make her more upset. The fact that she didn't realize it sooner did say a little bit about her life, but she was happy to have this kind of place here, and the different aspects of it definitely are good for her.

"Yeah, I'm glad that I have a means to leave. I knew that my mom was toxic, but I certainly didn't expect this," she said.

"I know. But you're happy you are doing the right thing Amelia, and you're strong. We'll make it through this together," Kayla replied.

Amelia nodded.

"Thank you Kayla. I do appreciate all that you've done for me. It's weird but...I've kind of fallen for you," Amelia said.

She felt dirty saying this right about now. She couldn't just hold this back for much longer. Amelia looked at Kayla, who seemed a bit flustered by this, but then, she nodded.

"I love you too Amelia. I love you a lot, but I'd rather talk to you about that after we're out of this whole mess. I don't feel it's right for you to stay," Kayla said.

Amelia agreed to that. Especially since her mom doesn't seem to have any desire to stop this anytime toon.

Whatever. Amelia wasn't her mother or anything. Fi she wanted to throw her life away, then so be it. She hoped that one day, her mother would stop being so damn toxic, but right now, she just wanted to spend her life with Kayla. She wanted to be with her, even if things got awkward. She knew that Kayla cared a lot about her, and she knew that Kayla felt the same way about Amelia as she did.

The comfort, the solace, all of that certainly made Amelia feel happy and secure. There was a lot going on right about now, and a lot that was eating away at Amelia, but she knew that being with Kayla like this was what mattered the most to her, and it was what made her feel better as well.

"We've got this. Together," Amelia said.

"We do," Kayla said.

They reached out, holding one another's hands for a second. There was still a lot that they needed to focus on, and a whole lot that was still at bay, but for Amelia, when she walked out of that house without saying goodbye, she felt strangely nervous about the future, but at the same time, she was also quite happy at the life that she had currently.

Things were rough, but Amelia was happy that she at least had her by her side, and she was sure that Kayla felt the same way.

They'd make it through this. Together.

Chapter Sixteen

Kayla felt awkward the entire time she was with Amelia in that home.

She could sense that Amelia's mother didn't really love her. It was very obvious from the way she acted. Still, Kayla wondered if the whole "I'm just trying to help you" mentality that she had was better, or worse than the one her dad had.

It was up for debate, that's for sure.

Amelia wondered at this point what was about to happen next, and what may transpire from all this. On the one hand, she was just happy that things were getting better for both of them, but at the same time, Amelia and she had a lot to discuss.

One of them was the feeling that they were both in love with one another.

Amelia was such a wonderful woman, and Kayla wanted nothing more than the best for her. She went through so much. While Kayla had the same problem, Amelia definitely deserved this just as much as she did.

After they got out of there, Amelia stopped, looking at Kayla for a second. Kayla wanted to just get the living hell out of here, but at the same time, she knew that there was something eating away at her.

"You good?" Kayla asked.

"Yeah. More than good. Thank you. For everything Kayla. I appreciate all that you've done," Amelia said.

Kayla nodded, looking at her with a nod.

"Very well. I'm glad that I'm here for you," Kayla said.

Amelia nodded, letting out a sigh.

"I'm sorry you had to see my mom like that. It's definitely not easy for me either," she admitted.

"Yeah. I'm glad that I'm here for you," Kayla replied.

She really was happy. She wanted to protect Amelia through all this.

"Do you think she's going to bother you?" Kayla asked. That was her biggest concern. She didn't know how things would pan out at this point. She wanted to take care of Amelia as best as she could.

"I honestly don't know for sure, Kayla. I'm a bit worried about it all, " Amelia said.

"Yeah. There's quite a lot of things going on," Kayla replied.

"Yeah, that's putting it lightly. I'm worried about what this means for all of us. There is a lot of things going on, but I just want to be happy. But, when I'm with you, I am. Anyway, let's get the hell out of here," Amelia said.

Kayla nodded, agreeing to this. There was a lot they could say, but Kayla wasn't comfy discussing this all the way out here. When she finally got the car started, she looked at Amelia, who seemed sad. She had tears in her eyes, but Kayla knew why.

"You're sad to see her go. Especially on these terms," she said.

"Yeah, but I don't want to go back to that life. I want to be free, and I feel stronger just leaving her place. So, thank you Kayla. Thanks for staying with me," she said.

"You're most welcome," Kayla replied.

It definitely was making things better for both of them. She liked the fact that she could spend this time with her, and she could be the person that she wanted to be.

She was better this way, and Kayla knew that she would do whatever it was that she could with her.

Everything was quite a challenge, but Kayla would do whatever it took to make Amelia happy. Even if things were a bit awkward at first, she was definitely ready to bring the happiness over to the table.

They drew back in silence, neither of them knowing what to say. Amelia had her own thoughts and Kayla just wanted to let her have her own feelings, let them simmer there and work together. But she also knew that no matter what they did next, Amelia was out of that toxic home.

When they got to Kayla's place, she immediately opened the door, showing Amelia the space.

"It's a pretty decent living space you can help with paying rent and such if you're cool with that," she said.

Amelia nodded.

"Of course. I want to help. I just wanted to get away from that," she admitted.

"Yeah, I don't blame you. It definitely is quite a bit of a challenge for both of us," she said.

Amelia seemed to understand that. With the way things were, both of them were just better off working on themselves, rather than succumb to the whims of other people. It was a mess, but she was just happy to have Amelia here with her.

After Amelia put her bags down, she knew for a fact that there was something they both needed to discuss. She sat down on the couch, and shortly after that, they looked at one another, and for a second, Amelia paused.

Kayla wondered what it was that she wanted to say. Perhaps it had something to do with the fact that Amelia was nervous about a few things. Maybe it was her own fear of the unknown, but then, Amelia took a deep breath.

"I'm glad that you're here with me Kayla. And when I told you that I loved you back there, I meant that," she admitted.

Kayla understood that feeling. She in fact felt the same way. It was different from what she was used to, and there was something about this which made Kayla nervous.

But she'd be lying if she didn't feel the same way.

Kayla wanted to say this for a while, but she wondered what might happen if she did admit all of this. She didn't know if Amelia felt the same way, at least till now.

"I do feel the same way Amelia. I just was nervous to pursue anything until after the fact. This is definitely good to know though. I'm happy, that's for sure," Kayla admitted.

It was a different feeling of happiness that would change the way things would be for both of them. Amelia did have her back, and she would have Amelia's, no matter what life would throw at them. Amelia blushed, but then, after a little bit, she spoke.

"So...we can work together though this?" she asked.

"I'd love that Amelia. I know life isn't easy for you, and I know you've been through a lot. I got word that my dad tried to get a bail. But they're not letting him do that. So, I don't have to worry about him. But...I want to take care of you. I want you to live your own life, even after all this. We'll work together, through it all, and I promise, I'll protect you like how I did that night," she admitted.

Kayla felt happy about that. She felt like it was her job to protect Amelia, even if things got out of hand. Amelia smiled, feeling grateful about it all

"Thank you Kayla. I know that I can trust you. You've...you've changed me for the better, and I'm happy about that," she admitted.

"If you ever need anything, you can always ask for me to help," she insisted.

They were in this together, able to work together, and able to be together. Amelia was the one person she cared about in life more than herself, and when Amelia looked at her with those eyes, Kayla felt her heart thump, and her body tense up slightly.

"You're okay?" Amelia asked.

Kayla nodded, feeling as if everything would change for the best. Even if they had to work through more problems, it would all be okay.

"Yeah. I have you by my side, and that's enough for me," she said.

Amelia nodded, smiling at her.

"Very well. I'm here for you too," she replied.

Amelia leaned in, pressing her lips to Kayla's. Kayla felt like she was on top of the world, able to live the life she wanted, and she'd do her best to protect Amelia, life be dammed. They kissed passionately, neither wanting to move. Amelia seemed happy, and Kayla pulled her in, touching her back. She would do whatever it took to make Amelia happy, and Kayla couldn't help but feel refreshed, happier, and full of life.

No matter what, they'd work together, and deep down, everything would be okay.

Chapter Seventeen

For a long time, Amelia didn't want to break contact. She felt sure, she felt happy, and the safety and the security that she felt when she kissed Kayla made her realize that there was good in the world, a bit of happiness in the darkness of the storm.

That was enough to keep Amelia going.

She felt like she should spend a little more time being upset by everything, but there was no time in that. She needed to stay positive, and to work through it.

They kissed for a long time, with Amelia moving toward Kayla's lap, kissing her with an unbridled passion. Kayla let out a small moan in response, which Amelia took advantage of.

Tonight, she wanted to make Kayla feel good.

Although they haven't had that much sex, there was something alluring about making out with Kayla that made Amelia feel happy and secure. As they pressed their lips together, making out and touching their tongues against one another, she straddled Kayla, pushing her body against hers. The grinding sensation that she felt made Amelia want more, and as she pushed her tongue there, brushing with Kayla's own and caressing there, she felt her body grow hot, the desire increasing over time.

Kayla then pressed her tongue against the tip, causing Amelia to let out a small shiver of pleasure, the excitement of it all growing within her. Kayla pressed her tongue down her neck, peppering little kisses, but then, Amelia responded back, doing the same thing and nibbling on the skin of her collarbone.

The sensation was enough to make Kayla let out a hiss of pleasure, and Amelia felt a sense of happiness and pride as she did that. Amelia could tell that Kayla was enjoying this just as much as she was, and soon, before she knew it, she had Kayla down on the couch.

Being on top of Kayla made Amelia feel powerful. She felt like she was in control, in her own little way, and when she looked down at Kayla, who was smirking at her, Amelia definitely felt a sense of wellness and pride at the moment.

"You good?" Kayla asked.

"Yeah. I want to make you feel good tonight," she said.

Amelia then moved her hands to Kayla's shirt, gripping the tip of it and moving it all the way upwards. She looked at Kayla, who was flushing slightly as Amelia pulled it all the way off, looking at Kayla's body.

She was thick, but in all the right places. With large, succulent breasts, a little hint of abs, and even just the thick thighs that she had there, she couldn't help but love the fact that Kayla looked at her like this, so vulnerable and ready for action.

Amelia definitely was ready for this. She couldn't help but feel like she was about to experience a whole lot of fun, and she was ready for every minute of it.

Amelia then moved her lips down toward Kayla's breasts, touching and teasing them there with subtle touches and licks. Kayla let out a small gasp, shuddering in response to Amelia's motions. Amelia smiled at Kayla, feeling a sense of pride, and even though she was definitely not sure what would happen next, she felt ready for whatever would happen between them. Kayla didn't seem to have any urge to top at the moment though, which surprised even Amelia.

She thought that Kayla would at least want to try. But Amelia wasn't complaining, so she pressed her lips downwards, touching the very edge of her breast. Amelia moved her hands to Kayla's bra, touching the back of the clasp. With one snap, she watched as the garment tumbled down, exposing Kayla's large orbs. Amelia was completely transfixed by all this, looking at the large orbs in anticipation as she moved her hands upwards, touching them slightly.

"Ahh," Kayla said, letting out a super cute, but low moan. Amelia smiled as she moved her hands up to Kayla's breasts, massaging them. She then started brushing her fingers over the tips of it. Amelia watched as Kayla arched her back, letting out a series of little sounds and moans. Everything about this was making Amelia feel the excitement and desire, making her crave more, and making her want this.

Amelia then pressed her tongue toward the tip of the nipple, touching the very tip of it with a little kiss of the lips. She sucked on the nipple, letting her other hand move toward the neglected bud, letting her fingers dangle there as she looked at Kayla with a smile on her face.

The whole thing was enough to drive Amelia mad, and she could feel her own body aching for more. She then flicked her tongue there, pulling slightly harder, and when she did that, Kayla started to let out a cry, arching her back and moaning in response to everything.

"Fuck," she said.

"Are you good?" Amelia asked.

"Yeah. Beyond good. I'm quite happy," she said.

Amelia couldn't help but feel a bit better about this she knew she was doing the right thing, and even just teasing Kayla was enough to get her going.

Amelia's lips and hands continued to dance on her skin, pulling on her nipples, and then shortly after touching the edge of Kayla's breasts, seizing the nipples and pressing against there. This alone was enough to make Kayla start to cry out, and everything about this was definitely making Amelia hot with need, flushing in desire, and she loved watching Kayla lose control at the present moment.

With every touch, with every press, with every moan, both of them grew hotter and hotter, the need increasing, until finally, Kayla flipped the whole scenario, pushing Amelia down. They kissed with a passion, Kayla' hands moving toward Amelia's body, undoing her clothing and tossing it to the side. She proceeded to kiss and suck on Amelia's soft skin too, both of them enjoying the sensation of the other person at the present moment.

Amelia didn't know how much more of this she could take. With every single moment, every single option, and every single touch, she knew that there was a need for so much more from Kayla.

Kayla then stepped back, looking at Amelia for a second.

"I need to grab something. Care to stick around here for a bit," she offered.

Amelia nodded, feeling the heavy anticipation for so much more grow within her. she watched as

Kayla left the room, only to return a few moments later with something.

It was a double ended dildo.

Amelia had seen them before in porn, but she didn't expect this from Kayla of all people. Kayla smiled and Amelia flushed in response as she took the towy, pushing Amelia's pants downwards, and then sliding the toy against her entrance.

When she did that, Amelia let out a cry, suddenly feeling her body grow hot was she felt it move in. Kayla pressed her lips against Amelia's heat too, pushing her tongue there and making Amelia cry out in response.

Every single moment in time, every pressing second, every single breath they took was bring Amelia closer and closer to the edge, her body hot with anticipation.

Soon, Kayla pulled back, looking at Amelia once again and Amelia gave a weak smile.

"Don't worry, I want this. Get over here," she said.

Her body was weak with desire, the feeling of the toy clenching against her insides making Amelia lose her mind. All of the control that's she had was certainly making her feel even more shocked by it all. It was a sensation that made her want nothing more than to just completely lose it, and feel the sudden passion grow out there.

Amelia loved this. She felt Kayla press herself on top of Amelia, sliding down there and looking at Amelia with a smile. Amelia let out a cry, and soon, their bodies were right up against one another. Kayla moved on top of Amelia, and she soon kissed Amelia.

Amelia was hungry for her. she kissed Kayla back, thrusting her hips up. When the toy stuck Kayla in that sweet spot, and Kayla cried out, suddenly rutting her hips against Amelia's own body. The whole thing was driving Amelia crazy, and she had no idea how much more of this she could take.

The feeling of wrought desire, the passion that she experienced, it was all so good, and for Amelia, almost too good to hold back. They started moaning, trying out one another's name against one another as they pressed their bodies against one another harder and harder, faster and faster.

After a few more moments Kayla pressed her hand against Amelia's spot, and when she rubbed there, Amelia let out a small, guttural sound. After a brief second, she then tensed up, holding herself there, and then, she started to let out a cry, and then she relaxed.

For a long time, she stayed there, looking at Kayla, whose body did the same. She then collapsed right over Amelia, pulling out the toy and discarding it to the side.

Amelia cuddled up in her arms, feeling safe and secure.

"Everything okay?" she asked Amelia.

Amelia did feel great. She was happy about it all, ready for action, and ready to be stronger than ever. She did feel good about this, and happy that she could have this moment with the woman she loved.

"Yeah, I'm wonderful. I'm...I'm doing a lot better than I thought I would. I feel like I can finally get my life together too without any problems," Amelia said.

She felt sure about that. She wasn't held back any more from the problems of her past, and when she looked at Kayla, who smiled at her, she felt a strange feeling of pure, unadulterated happiness.

"I'm glad that I have you. Together, we'll make our way through this," she said.

"Yeah, we sure will," Amelia said.

They kissed one another, both of them making out for just a little bit before they cuddled for a bit, falling asleep in one another's arms. It was the beginning of a new, and brighter future, and for both of them, they were definitely happy with this. It was only a matter of time, and for Amelia, she felt like even if things did get awkward for a bit, she at least had Kayla here with her to help support her through all this.

Chapter Eighteen

Kayla was happy.

For the first time in a long time, she truly, utterly did feel happy. Even with the stress of everything right now, she felt happy and satisfied by it all. She didn't have to worry about her dad coming back into the picture.

For the next three months, everything felt like a blur. Amelia was one of the top dancers out at the club, and Amelia seemed happy.

For Kayla, the club became one of the most popular in the city, with more and more people coming to it. Kayla was happy, but she also felt like this growth was unprecedented.

"I can't believe another article reported on this place," she said to herself as she finished the article. However, there was an email that made Kayla look at it with concern.

"What is that?" she said.

She opened the email, reading it.

Hello Kayla, I hope you're well,

I'm writing you today because I wanted to inquire about the chance of acquiring your property. I'm an investor, and I'd love to work with you. I hope we can do business together.

Best,

Ken

Another one. Kayla scoffed as she looked at the email. It was another investor trying to cash in on the fact that she had a club which was mildly successful. She wondered if she should say something about it.

Kayla called Mandy, and invited her in. The brunette stepped inside, slipping into the chair on the other side, across from Kayla.

"Something the matter? You look worried," she said.

"Yeah, sorry about that. Just a little bit perplexed, that's all," Kayla said.

"About what? The club is doing amazing by the way," she said.

"Yeah, that's the problem. I'm happy that we are, but it seems like these damn investors think I want to sell to them. I have zero desire to," Kayla said, showing the email to Mandy.

As soon as Mandy saw it, she cringed.

"Not another one!"

"What do you mean?" Kayla asked.

Mandy furrowed her brows, looking at Kayla with a serious look.

"I can't believe there's another person out there who is trying to buy up our space. I can't do that!" she said.

Kayla nodded, listening to her.

"I know. That's what worries me the most," she admitted.

"Yeah well, the feeling is mutual Kayla. I'm just shocked, that's all," she said.

"You and me both. So, what should we do? I mean, we could either just write them a letter back or—"

Mandy shook her head, listening to Kayla's words.

"No. You don't do that," Mandy insisted.

You don't? Kayla looked at Mandy with widened eyes, and a puzzled frown.

"What do you mean?" she asked.

"What I mean is, you just don't go and do that. You need to actually show these guys that you're here to stay, that you're not planning on leaving or anything. I for one think maybe we should hold an event here. Not with the dancers, but maybe like a gala or something. Invite the regulars and such," Mandy explained.

"That's a great idea," Kayla said, looking at Mandy with a beaming grin. It made total sense in a way.

"Yeah, so let's plan something," she replied.

Kayla felt good about it all and thought that planning this was the best solution.

After all, maybe this could get the people off her back.

She looked at the news in the area once again, and then, she frowned.

"Who is saying I'm looking for a boyfriend?" she asked.

"Oh yeah. Some guys were asking. They keep offering good money and stuff, but I tell them you're not interested," Mandy replied.

Kayla scoffed.

"Because I'm gay and have a girlfriend. Jesus," she muttered.

"How is that by the way? Things good with her?" Mandy asked.

Kayla nodded.

"She's the best goddamn thing to have happen to me. I'm glad that I have her. she makes this all much easier on me," she admitted.

"Good. I'm glad about that. I can tell you've got a lot going on and all," she pointed out.

Kayla did have to admit that it certainly was the case. She then started to sigh. She needed to clear these rumors up, and it certainly was quite important.

"All right. Let me put together an invite and everything," she said.

"Good. If you need anything let me know," Mandy said.

She walked off, leaving Kayla alone. She sighed, feeling flustered by this. She wanted to clear the air, but she also wanted to be honest about the feelings she had. She was sick of hiding them, and she certainly was quite better off as well.

Kayla finished the invite, and as she sent them out, her phone rang.

"Hello?" she stated.

"Hey , it's me," Amelia replied.

"Oh, hey? You coming in tonight? It's your off night though," Kayla pointed out. She checked the calendar and that was the case.

"Yeah well, something changed. I need to go see my mom," Amelia said.

Her mom? But why?

"Why is that?" Kayla said.

"She messaged me. Told me that she wants to talk. I guess she's trying to come around," Kayla said in response.

She didn't know if Amelia should trust her mom's words.

"I want to see her Kayla. Don't worry, I'll be okay," Amelia insisted.

"All right. Also, I wanted to let you know we are having a gala here on the 22nd, so we do need to clean the place up to make it impeccable," Kayla said.

"Very well. I'll talk to you later."

The phone clicked off, and Kayla sighed. There was a lot going on at the moment and she didn't know how to fully process all this. But, Kayla tried her best, and with the way everything was, it certainly was better that they worked through it all together.

She just needed those damn investors off her back.

Chapter Nineteen

Amelia felt fear the moment she got the call asking to meet up at the local coffee shop.

Her mother didn't want to meet in private thankfully, but the fact that she wanted to meet up at all was cause for alarm for Amelia. There was a lot happening in her life right now that she didn't know what to do about, except of course, to just let things happen as they happen.

But, when Amelia got there, she saw her mom. She had bloodshot eyes, like she'd been crying. She waved for Amelia to come over, and when Amelia did, her mother smiled.

"Thank God you're here. I thought you would've ignored me," she admitted.

"I wanted to hear what you had to say," Amelia said.

"Well, first of all I'm very sorry for everything that I said to you. Back then. I really, really am," her mother started.

Amelia tensed, feeling all the blood rush around her body. She didn't know how to cope with any of this. She felt as if there was some sort of force holding her there. She was frightened and unsure of what to do about any of it.

"What's the matter?" Amelia asked, noticing her mom looking downcast.

"I made some stupid decisions Amelia. Very stupid decisions," she admitted.

Amelia paused, trying to figure out what to do at this moment in time. She wanted to hear about this, and she wanted to see if there was anything she could do at this point.

"What's the matter? What kinds of decisions? I mean, you did kick me out of the house, and you didn't accept my relationship, but something bigger happened," Amelia said.

Her mother looked away, sighing in frustration.

"I screwed up," her mother simply said.

"What did you screw up on, Mom? Seriously, what the hell is going on," Amelia asked.

"Well, I kicked you out because I thought Cody and I could be together. Then I realized we can't," she said.

Amelia paused, feeling a bit unsure of things. She didn't know if her mom meant it or not.

"What do you mean? What did he do to you?" Amelia asked.

"Oh Amelia. It was awful. I can't believe he did what he did. He cheated on me with someone who was as young as he was. He's been seeing other women despite wanting a monogamous relationship. If I knew he was such a piece of garbage, I would've just left it at that," she muttered.

Ame;oa knew that he was a scumbag, but she also felt like her mom kind of deserved that one.

"I'm sorry Mom. But you now understand right? How when you treat someone like garbage it hurts more than just them? It's hard for me to forgive you for what you did," she admitted.

Amelia didn't like that. She felt hurt by the way her mom acted, the actions at hand, and how it all transpired. She was definitely upset about the way her mom did her dirty in the past. But, seeing her like this now hurt just as much.

"Do you understand what you did Mom? Do you understand how I feel? how you don't accept my life even though I've tried to do what's best for me?" Amelia asked.

Her mother looked at Amelia with concern, and after a brief moment, she nodded.

"Yeah. I do. I get that Amelia. I'm just not sure what this means for us. I don't really condone same-sex relationships. They're wrong," her mother replied.

Amelia clenched her fingers on the table. Her mom has quite a way of making her feel horrible. Amelia threaded her fingers through her red hair, looking at the woman who bore her. She wanted to just lash out, to tell her mom that she was wrong, and she didn't understand. Instead, she took things slowly.

"Listen, Mom. I understand your problems. I understand the stress you're under. But you have to understand. I know it's weird for you, but I'm not going to change. I love her Mom, and she loves me," Amelia replied.

Her mother looked at Amelia with slight disgust. After a brief moment, she nodded.

"Very well. I can't ever tell you to not love someone. I may be your mom, but you also live your own life. While I don't support the concept in general, if she does make you happy, then that's all that matters," her mother stated.

Amelia nodded.

"She does. Mom. She really, truly does make me happy. More than a lot of people actually," Amelia replied.

She never felt the way she did before, but when she thought about Kayla, things made sense. Her heart fluttered in response, and Amelia was definitely a bit relieved by all this.

"You're a good kid. I'm glad that I raised you correctly. And I guess I'm jealous, Amelia. Of you," her mother replied.

Jealous? Of her? Why would she be?

"But why Mom?" Amelia asked.

"Because you found happiness. I sometimes wish I could say the same. But, I haven't. I thought I did with your father, but he was a bastard who left you when you were just a child. I've wanted that for you, not because I feel like an irresponsible parent, but because I feel I at least owe you that," she said.

Amelia understood that. She did feel a little bit sad that she never got to have the childhood she wanted.

"I'm glad that you understand that. I do wish sometimes dad stuck around, but you did your best at raising me, even with all of this," Amelia replied.

Her mother sighed, looking at Amelia directly in the eyes.

"I also accept your job. As much as I don't like you putting yourself out there, I'm your mom, not the boss of your life. Do what makes you happy. If that's what does, then continue to do that," she admitted.

Amelia's eyes widened in shock. She couldn't believe that her mom actually wanted her to do that.

"Are you sure, Mom?" she asked.

"Does it look like I'm saying no, Amelia? Of course, I want that. You deserve the best, and you deserve to take care of yourself. I'm not going to sit there and control your life. You need to understand that. As much as I dislike something, I can't control it. And it pays your bills, right?"

Amelia nodded.

"More than that," she admitted.

"Then continue to do that. Work toward your dream, but also have something you can fall back on," her mother replied.

Amelia felt a bit of relief as she listened to her mother's words. She couldn't help but feel good about this, and she was a bit relieved by it all.

"Thank you, Mom. Even if you don't like this, that you're here for me. It's quite refreshing," Amelia admitted.

"I mean, someone has to be there for you, right?" her mother said with a smile.

"Yeah. Anyway, I'm glad you're supportive. We may not get along, but I'm here for you," she replied.

Amelia felt good and happy. She didn't feel like she was burdened as she should be.

"Thanks Mom. I love you," Amelia replied.

After they finished their drinks, they parted ways. Amelia learned from her mom that there was a lot going on in her life, and she'd be working, but she said she was always open to talk.

They agreed to see one another again in the coming weeks, and Amelia wanted to be near her mom. But it certainly was a bit of a strange situation.

Least she wasn't mad anymore. They ended on friendly terms, and although amicable, Amelia still felt off even just being near her.

Chapter Twenty

Kayla and Amelia met to discuss the whole plan for the gala, but of course, Kayla was curious about something else.

"So, what did your mom want?" she asked.

Amelia flushed, then spoke.

"Well, my mom basically told me she was sorry. I don't know if I fully trust her again, but I do believe that it's something that we can work on. She does seem to accept us," Amelia replied.

Kayla nodded. although she didn't believe it herself, she at least tried to humor her girlfriend.

"I'm glad that you two worked it out. Just be careful, okay," Kayla said.

Amelia nodded.

"Don't worry, I don't fully trust my own mother yet either. I know that she means well, but damn, it feels so weird hearing her like this," Amelia said.

"Yeah well, that's how people are. I guess your mom feels a little guilty. But we have each other. I think we'll be okay," Kayla said.

Amelia nodded.

"Yeah, we will be. Thanks for being there for me Kayla. I'll be there for you through all of this," Amelia replied.

Kayla didn't want to think about the gala. She already had a feeling so many big names would be there, asking for her to sell the club.

"Yeah, I'm going to need it. This is going to be annoying to deal with. But I feel once we get this sorted out, we can finally live our own life," Kayla said.

Amelia beamed, agreeing to that.

"I'm glad about that," she replied.

"Anyway, I guess it's time to figure out how we want to set this place up. We can go dress shopping together too," Kayla said.

The two of them went dress shopping, both finding dresses that fir their looks. Kayla got a slinky black dress that accentuated her curves, while Amelia meanwhile had a red minidress that showed off her long legs.

The two planned to get dressed together, and on the day of, decorators came in, sprucing the place up and cleaning it.

"This looks great," Amelia said as she looked around.

"Yeah, I'm glad that we managed to get this to look right. I was a bit worried myself," Kayla replied.

They finished cleaning and preparing just as the first guests came in. Kayla looked at Amelia, who was helping to serve people drinks and appetizers. Kayla felt proud of the place that she put together.

As more and more of the investors came in, each with dates, they all said hello to Kayla. A couple of them shook Kayla's hand for a little longer than she anticipated. After the last of the people came in, mingling with others, Kayla went behind the stage they had. The women were out there, serving drinks and appetizers to everyone. But Amelia noticed Kayla's face.

Kayla was nervous.

"You okay there?" Amelia asked as she walked over.

"Been better. A lot of the bigwigs showed up. I want you to come up there with me. I want to inform every one of you. If that's okay," Kayla said.

Amelia blushed, but then she nodded.

"I'd love to help you Kayla. I can see you need it," Amelia admitted.

Kayla was thankful for that. She gave Amelia a kiss on the lips and then walked behind the curtain. A couple of other people spoke, some of them talking about this establishment, and others about the entertainment. While it was a gentleman's club, it only brought in the more affluent of people. Kayla was just happy to have such a nice establishment.

When it was time for Kayla to go up on stage, the emcee, one of the dancers, introduced her. Kayla walked up, smiling at everyone with a grin.

"Good evening everyone. I'm happy to have all of you gathered here today in celebration of the strides that we made. Everything is quite different, and I'm glad that we are able to produce such a great and wonderous place. But I do have to say, there are a few rumors I'd like to clear up before we continue. Nothing big, just a few rumors about not only myself, but also about the club at hand," Kayla started.

The people all around looked at her with slight surprise, and Kayla sighed. She knew that this was something that she'd need to handle, and stat.

"Anyway, I'm here to talk to you about the state of this club. I've gotten countless emails recently asking if the club was for sale, or if we'd like to talk business. I'm here to dispel those rumors," Kayla started.

The people around looked at her with slight surprise, and then, Kayla spoke.

"I have no intent of selling the club right now. I'm not sure how many of you know, but I built this from the ground up. As a victim of abuse, I run this club as a haven for dancers from harmful people, both male and female, and I want women to work in a place where they are safe and empowered. I feel having it under new management defeats that purpose, so I will not be selling this place anytime soon," Kayla started.

The people around started to look at her, and then whisper a few words here and there. Kayla knew this was coming, and she was ready for the fallout.

"I'm sure some of you are asking where you can put your money at now, since I have zero desire to sell the club. Well, the answer to that is simple: other businesses. Look to see who is selling, and from there, offer to them. They are more in the market than I am, since I love my club, and this is kind of like my baby. I don't want to let this go by the wayside," Kayla explained.

The people made a bit of noise at those words, but it wasn't like Kayla didn't expect it. She simply nodded.

"I know you're not all that happy about this but…I'm serious, this is what I plan to do. I'm going to continue like this. Also, there is another matter I'd like to attend to. It's about my relationship status. I know some of you have been asking if I have a boyfriend, or if I want to be in a relationship. Well, I'm going to come forward and clean about things. For starters, I'm not interested in men. Second of all, I have a partner. Come here Amelia," Kayla said.

Amelia shuffled on forward, looking at Kayla with widened eyes.

"This is my partner Amelia. Amelia, this is everyone. I'm sure that they all understand, but I have zero desire for anyone else in the world besides you. Amelia has been with me since the beginning, and I'm glad that I have her right now. I know that...it's a bit different for us, but please learn to understand," Kayla said.

The people did talk a bit, but Kayla watched as Amelia took the podium.

"I love her. she's my rock, and we work so well together. I know this may not be ideal for everyone, but please, try to respect our relationship," Amelia said.

Everyone seemed to say a few words, and Kayla felt a bit worried about things, but she was happy as well that Amelia was willing to talk to them. After they finished there, Amelia followed Kayla over to the back of the club.

"You think it'll be okay?" Amelia asked.

"Yeah, I think so. It's different, but I'm sure that most people will understand," Kayla said.

Sure enough, people did. A few people came to offer their support. Some were upset, but most people supported them as the kickass power couple. Kayla was relieved about that. She worried how things would be if she did not have that support.

But she was happy. She had Amelia by her side, and they were in love. They could face the unknown together, and for Kayla, she had a feeling that no matter what happened in the future, they'd make it through together, and build a better, stronger life than they had in the past.

www.ingramcontent.com/pod-product-compliance
Lightning Source LLC
LaVergne TN
LVHW010611160826
845677LV00013B/3369
* 9 7 9 8 6 6 7 9 0 2 7 8 2 *